THEIR DUCHESS

THEIRS
BOOK TWO

JESS MICHAELS

For Michael. You make the ship go and I could not be me without you.

PROLOGUE

Summer 1812

Anna

The moment when the Duchess of Sedgewick could watch her husband fuck his mistress without her heart breaking was the moment she knew her marriage was truly over.

It wasn't that the feeling hadn't been a long time coming. She and Sedgewick had never been a love match, even if Anna had once had a brief hope that they could come to some warmth and affection with each other.

But they hadn't. And in the last five years of their six-year marriage, they'd been coming together to the Donville Masquerade, an erotic underground club where members could explore their deepest desires. At first it had been to watch, an aphrodisiac, he had told her. Then to play together—a rather half-hearted attempt on his part.

Eventually he'd turned to other women and even encouraged her to seek her own pleasure. She had never born him children, ; she was not capable. He, apparently, was, because several of his mistresses had his by-blows. He had smiled at her, almost warmly, and pointed out that he had no fear of bringing "polluted blood" into his line from her dalliances. Though she had no strong desire for children one way or another, the casualness of that remark had stung.

They'd even looked into divorce, but the laws were difficult and the freedom wouldn't be worth the huge scandal to Sedgewick and his family. No, he had surrendered himself to the idea that his young brother's sons would inherit his title and that he could have his mistresses and courtesans. He only seemed to hate her a little for the former and the latter no longer felt like a punishment.

So they lived together in faint misery, growing further apart with each passing day.

Anna momentarily dropped her gaze away from the little spying window that peered into the room where Sedgewick and his latest lover were tangled in each other. The Donville Masquerade allowed for watching if couples wanted it. This dark hall peered into many a room. Anna had simply made the mistake of looking into this one.

The woman with Sedgewick gave a side glance to the window, as if she knew she was being watched and liked it. What was her name again? Lydia? Laura? Anna couldn't recall. It didn't matter anyway. She was blonde and beautiful and younger than the duchess, who had just watched her twenty-eighth year expire.

Anna sighed and moved into a dark corner of the corridor to collect herself, only instead of finding a wall to lean on, her fingers met a solid, warm chest. She gasped and the man cloaked in darkness sucked in a breath.

"Forgive me," he said, his voice low and rough in the darkness. It sent a delicious shiver through her body and made heat settle between her legs. No man's voice had ever affected her so instantly and powerfully.

"N-no, pardon me," she said, her voice trembling as she slowly drew her hand away from him. "I didn't see you there."

"I should have made my presence known," he said. "I will go."

He moved to do so. The light from the little spy area where she'd been watching Sedgewick hit his form and let her see the shape of the stranger. He was tall and broad-shouldered.

"Wait," she said, almost not meaning to speak.

He stopped immediately and turned to look at her, even though she doubted he could see her in the dark any more than she could see him. "Yes?"

"Were you watching me...or-or someone else?" Anna asked.

He cleared his throat. "You," he admitted softly. "I saw you in the hall and couldn't stop myself from following."

She caught her breath. "I see."

"You were watching a room," he said. There was no judgment in his tone, but there was a hint of tension.

She bent her head, glad he couldn't see her expression in the shadows. It made her...braver. As did the fact that he was a stranger and could never know who she was out in the world. She wore a mask here, after all, and now she was just a shadow to him, as he was to her.

"I was watching my...my husband," she explained. "Watching him take pleasures with someone else that he refuses to take with me any longer."

"Bastard," the stranger said with surprising heat to his tone considering he didn't know her. "Fool."

"How would you know?" she asked.

He hesitated but then moved toward her. She felt the gentle warmth of his minty breath caress her skin as he leaned down. "You are beautiful."

Her own breath was almost nonexistent now that he was so close. "I'm wearing a mask."

"I'd wager you wear many a mask. None of them hide your beauty."

"And you think that should be enough to make him…want me like he wants her?"

She felt the brush of rough fingers against her cheek, just below the mask they had been discussing. "There are a great many reasons why he should want you. Why, if you were mine, I would make sure you knew how much you were wanted."

"You know that, do you?" she gasped out, trying to be bolder than she felt when he was so close and there was so much crackling in the air between them. Some of it far deeper than mere desire.

"I've known it since the first moment I laid eyes on you," he said, his voice suddenly strained.

Anna's heart was pounding now, the blood rushing so loud in her ears that she couldn't hear anything else. But perhaps that was best because it dialed all the focus in her mind and body to the shadowy presence of the man before her.

She'd had lovers before. In this very club, in fact. Usually masked men who were as disconnected as her husband when they touched her. Sometimes there was pleasure. But she'd never experienced the kind of hungry, animal draw to anyone that she felt toward this man whose face and name she didn't even know.

"W-what if I *could* be yours?" she asked. "R-right here. Right now."

She heard his breath catch, felt the wobble of him like she'd weakened his knees with that suggestion. It was a heady thing since she could tell the man was powerful, even if she couldn't see him. Physically commanding, yes, but also someone who knew who he was and what he wanted. That he wanted her was a thrill.

"Are you certain you'd desire that?" he asked.

She felt the blood rush to her cheeks and was once again happy he couldn't see her humiliation when she said, "In this moment, I-I want to feel wanted. You say you could make that happen. And the Donville Masquerade is where people come for such things."

She stepped up to him, letting her hand find his chest a second time. Her palm flattened against the rough fabric of his jacket and she shivered as she slid her fingers up the hard expanse of him beneath it. Eventually she traced the line of his jaw. It was harsh and peppered with whiskers. Not in fashion, but she wanted to feel them brush against her skin nonetheless.

"I...need to tell you who I am," he began.

Anna shook her head. "Oh, please don't," she murmured. "This is a fantasy. A dream. If I know your identity, then it will make coming back into reality that much harder."

He hesitated for what felt like an eternity, like he was weighing the ethics of her suggestion. But then his arms came around her... steady, strong. She shivered against the warmth and width of him. Oh yes. She wanted this encounter in the dark. She wanted it more than she'd wanted anything in a very long time.

He dipped his head, the edges of their masks tapped and then his lips found hers. She was shocked at how he moaned when their mouths brushed, like he'd been waiting a lifetime for this moment. But she couldn't process that because he swiftly swept her away.

His tongue breached her mouth and he pivoted her so her back was to the wall. He kissed her with abandon, drinking her in, inhaling her. Ravishing her, but gently. She drowned in that, drowned in him, memorizing his taste and his touch so she could remember them later when she felt lonely and unwanted.

He deepened the kiss, slowed it, and she wound her arms around his neck, lifting against him, rubbing her breasts against his chest as she made a little moan that was lost against his seeking tongue.

He drew back. Anna felt him looking down at her shadow in the dark, calculating...well, what she couldn't say. He'd followed her into the back hallway, he knew why she was here and why he was here in this den of sin and pleasure. She'd offered herself and still he hesitated.

"Please," she whispered, whimpered, and hated herself for it.

"You deserve such pleasure," he murmured, almost as if to himself rather than her. "I want to give you such pleasure."

She stared, seeking his features, wishing for the first time that this encounter wasn't anonymous. She wanted to see his face, to read why he sounded so earnest in that desire. Like it mattered to him how she felt, if she came.

Had any man ever done that? And this one didn't even know her name.

"I—" she began, but didn't have a chance to finish.

He pressed his mouth back to hers, this time with more power, with more purpose. He flattened her against the wall, letting her feel the full length of him, the weight of him. His hands began to move over her, down her sides, around her waist, tucking her closer to him as she moaned against his mouth once more.

He dragged his lips away from hers, across her neck, sucking there lightly as she arched against him. Next he kissed her collarbone, the soft curve of the top of her breasts that was exposed in the revealing gown she'd worn here. His thumbs stroked against her ribcage, his hands drew down to her hips as he slowly went to his knees before her.

She couldn't breathe as she realized in that heated moment what he was about to do. He lifted her skirt, the cool air in the dark hallway hitting her calves, her knees as he shoved the silky fabric away. He palmed her thighs, spreading them slightly before his fingers found the place between them.

She wore no underthings and was shaved there, and he swore beneath his breath as he made those two discoveries for himself. Anna rested her head back against the wall, closed her eyes and smiled as she surrendered to this moment, to this stranger.

He pressed his mouth to her hip, down against the inside of her thigh, his whiskers lightly abrading the ultrasensitive skin. She gasped and dropped her fingers into his thick hair, massaging his scalp in encouragement as he peeled her open with his thumbs and pressed his mouth to her entrance.

She jolted as the wet heat of his tongue met her. He groaned against her, the vibration rippling through her as she gasped and began to grind against him. He stroked her, gentle at first, tasting every fold, devouring her like she was the finest feast. She lost herself in his touch, forgetting where they were, who she was, what she had seen in that room where her husband made love to some other woman.

Everything was this stranger and his tongue lapping her up and drawing pleasure from her that built with such intensity that she could only cling to him as she rode it.

He gripped her hips tighter as he grunted, like this was his own pleasure. Then his mouth moved away from her. "God, I want to do this all night. I want to tease you all night. But someone will enter this hall soon enough, it is inevitable, and I don't want this to have an audience."

She shivered and widened her stance, opening herself further so he could take her. "Then you should take your pleasure."

He hesitated. "You misunderstand me. I would draw out *your* pleasure for hours if I could. But instead..." He didn't finish the sentence, but instead returned his mouth to her pussy. He latched onto her clitoris and began to suck, swirling his tongue around her as he did so.

Electric pleasure arched immediately through her entire body, and she flailed against the wall, digging her hands into his shoulders. Her hips ground helplessly against his talented tongue, reaching for more, shaking for more.

And then she fell over the edge of intense sensation, her orgasm ripping through her as she wailed. She didn't care who heard her or who saw her or what happened next. All that mattered was this man's mouth and the magical things he was doing with it. Her orgasm felt like it went on forever, to the edge of pain, of madness. And only then did he draw away, kissing her thigh again, this time so gently that it almost brought tears to her eyes.

"That was everything I have ever dreamed of," he murmured, his low voice even rougher than before.

She blinked, her addled mind unable to fully process that statement. She tugged at him, pulling him to his feet and drawing him against her. She kissed him, tasting the salty sweetness of her release on his lips and tongue.

He leaned against her, the hard ridge of his erection patently clear against her belly. She rubbed against him, aching for more in a way she had never fully felt before.

But he didn't take her. To her surprise, he pulled away, his fingers gliding against her cheek before his hand dropped to his sides.

"Wh-why?" she whimpered, smoothing her gown back down over her body.

He let out a ragged sigh. "I wanted to give you pleasure. And I got to do that. I will live on that memory for the rest of my life."

"But I..." She shook her head and cut herself off. She'd spent far too much time begging her husband to care for her—she wasn't about to do the same with a stranger whose face she didn't even know.

"Please don't hate me," he whispered.

Anna caught her breath. "I couldn't. What you just did...it was wonderful. And I will also hold this memory dear."

He was silent a long moment, and she thought he might say more. That he might offer something beyond the pleasure he'd given. Instead, he leaned in and kissed her once more, this time with gentleness. A goodbye, and one that felt intensely bittersweet despite the fact they didn't even know each other.

"Thank you," he said softly.

Tears leapt to her eyes and she blinked them away. "Thank *you*," she whispered.

He released her and turned away. She watched his shadow

depart and then sagged against the wall where he had drawn such pleasure from her weak body.

And wished she was free to follow him and find out exactly who he was. But she wasn't. And knowing his face would only make things harder in the long run. At least that was what she told herself before she smoothed her skirts and left the hallway to return to her mundane, empty life as the Duchess of Sedgewick.

CHAPTER 1

Winter 1813

Oliver

Oliver Wynn gripped the reins tighter and knew it wouldn't help at all. He'd been a driver long enough to know when a situation was hopeless. They weren't going to make it. The rain had turned to ice, the roads were slick and treacherous and the cold was biting. Even through his thick gloves, his fingers felt frozen.

He could only imagine the Duchess of Sedgewick, his longtime employer, was little more comfortable in the carriage he drove. And if he didn't get them to someplace safe, her comfort would not be the problem. Her safety would be.

He squinted into the slashing rain and blinked against the weather. There in the distance were…lights. At least he thought they were lights. Perhaps it was just wishful thinking. But it was better than nothing, so he steered the exhausted horses in the direction of the faintest hope. It took longer than he wished. The mud was thick and icy, the animals could only go so fast, but at last they turned through a gate and up a winding drive toward a large manor house on a hill. Oliver could have wept with relief as he pulled the horses up and stretched his fingers. After gripping the reins so tightly in the last few hours of the journey, he could scarcely feel the digits.

He began to maneuver down from the top of the vehicle, being careful on the icy step, just as servants rushed toward the rig.

"Bad weather," one of them grunted as they took the reins of the horses.

"Nearly deadly," Oliver agreed. "I was relieved to see the house. Is your master at home?"

The stablehand nodded. "Oh yes. Mr. Pembroke is in residence. And I'm certain he will put your passengers up." The young man glanced over his shoulder toward the house. "There he is now. You may speak to him, yourself."

Oliver smoothed his sodden coat and moved toward the steps and the man who stood at the top of them. As he neared him, his breath caught. The master of this house was very handsome, indeed, with lightly graying dark blond hair and eyes so brightly blue that they were impossible not to look at. He had a strong jaw and full lips. It was an intelligent face. A commanding face.

He was casually dressed, with no jacket or cravat, likely because he wasn't expecting company in the middle of an ice storm. His sleeves were rolled to the elbow, and Oliver marked a slash of what appeared to be paint on one of the man's rippled forearms.

He shook off his reaction to the man and executed a polite nod. "I beg your pardon, my lord. The Duchess of Sedgewick is my passenger, and as you can see, we were surprised by the weather. I wonder if she might take refuge at your home for the night?"

The man in the doorway's gaze fluttered over Oliver in a slow, heavy glance that made every muscle in Oliver's body tighten with tension. Not unpleasant tension, more like awareness. Then he inclined his head.

"Of course," he said. "I would never allow Her Grace...or you... to freeze. Please, let my servants tend to your animals and carriage."

Oliver nodded. He was so cold and so tired from fighting the weather for hours, he could hardly think straight. The idea that someone else would take care of his duties was heavenly. "I will fetch Her Grace, then," he said. "Thank you, my lord."

The gentleman shook his head. "Pembroke," he said. "My grandfather is an earl, but I am no one's lord."

Oliver somehow doubted that was true, but he didn't argue and instead turned back toward the carriage. He drew a long breath before he opened the door and peered inside.

The Duchess of Sedgewick...Anna, beautiful Anna...was cuddled beneath a thick blanket in the corner of the rig. She looked at him with concern.

"Oh, Oliver," she said. "You look cold as ice."

"I'm fine," he lied. "Only sorry that my poor planning put us in such a situation. But we've arrived at the home of a Mr. Pembroke and the gentleman is willing to allow us to stop here for the night."

She shifted and he could see she was uncomfortable. Of course she would be. The man at the door was a stranger, for one. And the trip Anna was making was difficult as it was. Drawing it out likely only made it more so.

But she didn't say any of that. Instead she leaned forward and touched Oliver's gloved hand with her own. Thick layers of fabric separated them, but he still had to fight not to respond to that touch. "You did so very well. Thank you for taking care of me and getting me here safely."

He swallowed past a suddenly thick throat before he croaked out, "Come. Let me escort you over the ice to the house."

She nodded, though her blue eyes never left his. Her hand took his more firmly and she leaned on him as she carefully exited the carriage. The softness of her against his body put him on edge, despite the tenuousness of the situation. But then, he'd always been susceptible to all the ways she made him feel. He couldn't control that, even if he controlled everything else.

He got her to the top of the steps at last and she looked up toward their savior. Mr. Pembroke stared down at her, his piercing blue stare sweeping over her from the crown of her head to the tips of her boots and there was a moment where awareness crackled between them. Anna straightened up a little, tilting her head to examine at him more carefully.

And Oliver was both enthralled by the instant attraction that so clearly bound them as well as jealous. Jealous that she wanted this man, that he wanted her in return. That if they chose, they could be free to do something about it. And all Oliver had were memories.

"Mr…" she began.

"Pembroke, Your Grace," he said. "Ezra Pembroke."

"Pembroke," she repeated softly. "Why does that seem so familiar?"

"My grandfather is the Earl of Barrowfield," Pembroke said. "I assume we shared a ballroom or two before I left good Society several years ago."

She nodded. "Yes, I do recognize the earl's name." Oliver heard the slight tension in her voice. "Well, I do appreciate your kindness, Mr. Pembroke."

"Please come in out of the cold, both of you. My servants are already taking your things inside and will tend to the horses as you settle in." He stepped aside and let Anna pass, then Oliver. Oliver couldn't help but note how Pembroke's gaze followed her with obvious interest.

His jaw tightened. The last thing he wanted was to leave Anna with a man who was no better than the one she was heading to see in the first place.

"You must be exhausted after your long day," Pembroke said. "Shall I show you to your chamber first so you may have a moment to yourself before supper?"

Anna glanced back at Oliver, her dark eyes snagging his and holding there. She seemed nervous. Not afraid, but uncertain. He moved forward. "Would you like me to join you, Your Grace? To help you settle anything?"

She nodded. "Yes, Oliver, that would be appreciated."

Pembroke turned that bright blue gaze on Oliver with what could only be perceived as interest. Oliver was being read, it seemed, and he was too exhausted not to be an open book. Not that it mattered.

"Whatever pleases you, Your Grace," Pembroke said gently. "Please follow me."

He led them both up a long staircase and then down a brightly lit hallway. A door there was already open, and they stepped in to reveal a lovely room with a cozy fire already burning. Anna almost sagged with relief. "It's very nice, Mr. Pembroke. You really are too kind."

The gentleman inclined his head. "Are there other servants I should send to you?"

She glanced again at Oliver, like she was seeking out his steadiness. He tried to provide it by smiling gently at her. She drew a shaky breath. "No. It is only Oliver and me."

Pembroke's brow lowered in confusion and Oliver wanted desperately to step in front of Anna and protect her from the embarrassment her confession obviously caused. Since her husband's death, he had watched her sense of self-worth and dignity be stripped away, by cruel design, little by little.

And he hated every moment of it. Hated even more that he was in no position to stop it.

Pembroke said nothing to address that fact, though, only nodded. "Then I will leave you to prepare. If you have any need of assistance, just ring."

He held Oliver's gaze a moment, then backed from the room. Anna gripped the edge of the mattress when he was gone and let her breath out like she'd been holding it. "I'm so sorry, Oliver," she said.

He shook his head. "Why are you sorry, Your Grace? Not only was I the one driving, but I planned the trip. I should have—"

"Should have what?" she interrupted, her tone suddenly bitter. "We both know there were no options. The new Duke of Sedgewick has ensured that for his own reasons. There was no place we could have gone, nothing we could have done. You saved us from a terrible fate by spotting Mr. Pembroke's home in the dark and bringing us here. By convincing him to take it a lost, foolish woman."

Oliver took a step toward her. "Don't say that," he said softly.

She lifted her gaze, and for a moment her lips parted. Then she blushed and turned her face. "I...I see that my trunk is already here, which is wonderful. Mr. Pembroke's people do not hesitate. But..."

"But?" Oliver asked.

She blushed almost plum-colored and refused to meet his gaze. "I-I think I'm going to need some help. I wore this gown assuming we would make it to the new duke's estate tonight and that he could provide a servant to assist me in changing."

Oliver's mouth went dry. "Shall I...shall I call for someone?" he asked.

She was silent for a long moment, her hands gripping and releasing the edge of the coverlet. Then she lifted her gaze to him once more. "I really don't want more witnesses to my humiliation, Oliver. Will you unfasten me? I can do the rest. I have a gown here that I can do myself and I've gotten very good at fixing my own hair since my maids were stripped away from me one by one by that horrid man."

Oliver stared. "Unfasten you?"

She nodded. "It's not fair or proper, I know. But we both

know…" She trailed off and shook her head. "If you don't want to, I will figure something else out."

"I will," he said softly, and reached back to close the door.

Suddenly the cozy closeness of the room felt very plain. Even plainer when he moved around the bed to where she stood and slowly put her back to him. He could hear every shudder of her breath, every whisper of her damp clothing brushing against her legs when she moved.

Her hair was done loosely, and Oliver could hardly breathe as he lifted his hand and gently pushed the weight of it aside to reveal the first button of her gown. She caught her breath at his touch and he was torn back to a stolen moment in the past. One he tried to forget again simply because if he thought of it, he would do things they would both likely regret.

He steadied his suddenly shaking hands and unfastened the first button. She gripped the edge of the bed tighter with a soft sound in her throat. He unfastened the second button, breathing in the soft scent of her skin: lilac and citrus. Something so incredibly perfect that he could have sunk into it and her and never come out again.

He unfastened the rest of the buttons, noting that her chemise beneath looked a little thin. Thin enough that he could see the pink of her skin through the semi-translucent fabric. There was no denying how much he wanted her in that moment. How much he wanted to turn her around and kiss her. Touch her. Have her.

He blinked those thoughts away and backed up. "Do you need further help?"

His voice sounded so rough, and he cleared his throat in the hopes it would make the desire coursing through him a little less obvious.

She turned to face him, holding up the gown by pressing her hand to her chest. "No, I…I think I can manage the rest. Thank you, Oliver."

Her pupils were dilated, her own voice shaky, and she let her gaze move over his face slowly. He could see that the want he felt for her was reflected in her own desires. And that was heady.

It was also impossible. So he did the thing he had to do and jerked out a quick nod before he moved away from her, moved to the door, where he hesitated. "I am close by if you need me, Your Grace. If you don't feel safe, I will come."

She nodded. "Yes. You always do, Oliver. Good—good night."

He turned away, hard and unsatisfied and burning for her. What he needed was to find his chamber, take care of this erection that was making itself painfully known beneath his trousers, and then remember his place. Which was not in her bed. No matter how much he wished it could be.

CHAPTER 2

Ezra

It had been almost an hour since Ezra had been witness to the crackling tension between the Duchess of Sedgewick and her remarkably attractive driver, and yet he couldn't get it out of his mind. It stirred something in him, something that hadn't been awake for a very long time.

There was a soft sound at the door to the parlor behind him, and Ezra turned. His butler, Iverson, entered the room with a swift nod. "The Duchess of Sedgewick, sir."

He stepped away and the duchess entered the room. She was wearing a simple gown, one he noted she could likely fasten and unfasten herself. Why didn't she have a maid with her? What was the story? For the first time in a long time, he wished he was more aware of his grandfather and father's world. They would have known every detail of this lovely woman's fall. They would have cackled about it over supper even while they made lewd comments about her.

On second thought, Ezra was perfectly happy not having their words about her in his head. He would find out in his own way.

"Good evening," she said, her voice strained. Her gaze moved over him swiftly and her open face was entirely readable. She was interested in him. Perhaps because of the situation they found themselves in. But also because of something deeper.

"Good evening, Your Grace," he said, nodding Iverson away before he crossed to the sideboard and motioning to the plethora of fine spirits and wines gathered there. "What can I get you?"

She swallowed hard. "Sherry?"

He smiled. "Are you sure?"

She drew a deep breath and her shoulders relaxed a little at the gentle teasing. "Sherry," she repeated, this time with certainty.

He poured her drink and handed it over, noting how she shifted constantly in her discomfort. Like butterfly wings. "Supper will be ready in a short while," he said, and motioned to the settee before the fire. She took a seat and he chose to sit across from her in one of the leather chairs. The distance seemed to steady her a little and she gulped her drink restlessly.

"Again, I must thank you for your kindness in accommodating me at your home," she said.

He waved a hand. "You have thanked me enough, Your Grace. I couldn't let you and your driver freeze. You are most welcome here."

She nodded and stared into her glass. She seemed uncertain of what to discuss. Which left the topic up to him.

He leaned forward. "You were married to the late Duke of Sedgewick," he said.

She shifted again. Pain fluttered briefly over her expression. "Yes. He died a few months ago."

Ezra tried to read her emotional response to that fact, but it was the one thing she hid well. He couldn't tell if her pain was grief or something else. "I'm sorry," he said.

"Thank you."

He tilted his head and tried to snag her gaze. "It does leave me to wonder what makes you trek across the countryside in such weather with only a driver to accompany you."

Now her gaze jerked up to his, panicked. God, but she was lovely. He could only imagine she'd only be lovelier when she wasn't pulsing with fear.

"You are under no obligation to tell me," he said, leaning back and trying to make his own posture more relaxed so that she might follow suit. She ducked her chin and he wondered what was in that pretty head of hers. "And what about him?"

She looked at him again. "Him?"

"Your driver," he said, even though he thought they were both perfectly aware of what he meant.

"Oliver," she whispered. There was so much emphasis she put on those three syllables. So much weight to his name, like it meant something to her.

"Oliver," he repeated, tasting the name on his own tongue.

"He was my husband's driver." There was a faraway look to her expression suddenly. "He is…he has been my friend. My very dear friend since His Grace's death."

Ezra arched a brow at that admission. Not one many duchesses would make about a servant, he didn't think.

"A friend," he repeated slowly. "Then perhaps I should invite your *friend* to join us for supper."

Her eyes went wide. "I—what?"

"Would it make you more comfortable?" he pressed.

She shifted and the answer was clear on her face. It was yes. It was no. It was fascinating. He wanted to know more about it all. He wanted to peel the edges of this away until he understood it.

"I…"

The bell rang at that moment, signaling supper. He stood and motioned his hand toward the direction of the attached chamber. "Go into the dining room, my dear," he said gently. "And I will return shortly. With your friend."

She opened and shut her mouth, but didn't refuse him the

suggestion as she slowly got to her feet and moved toward the dining room. She didn't call him back as he strode from the room and down the hallway. Iverson was coming from the opposite direction and Ezra slowed.

"Where was Her Grace's driver put?" he asked.

Iverson blinked, confused by the question for a moment. "Mr. Wynn?" he asked.

Ezra chuckled. "If that is her driver."

"Er, the third floor, sir. Fourth door to the left. In the servant quarters." Iverson shifted. "Should I…should I fetch him? Is there a problem you need me to attend to?"

"I'm happy to fetch him myself," Ezra said, and began up the stairs. "And there is the complete opposite of a problem, I assure you. Have a place added for supper, will you?"

He could practically feel Iverson's confusion radiating off of him, but the servant didn't ask further questions. All of Ezra's staff were accustomed to his…idiosyncrasies. And to the private nature of those who were invited into this space. In that, Ezra trusted. And if things played out in the most interesting way, he'd be certain that the Duchess of Sedgewick knew it too.

He bounded up the backstairs into the servant area of the house and stopped at the door that Iverson had mentioned. He smoothed his jacket slowly before he rapped his knuckles on the surface. There was a rustling and then the door opened to reveal Oliver Wynn. The man had been in the process of changing, it seemed. He had a clean, dry shirt on, but it wasn't fully buttoned, so it revealed a v of extremely attractive chest. Muscular from work. His hair was wild, probably from the towel that was draped across his shoulder. Behind him, Ezra could see his sodden jacket and shirt spread out to dry before the small fire in the grate.

"Mr—Mr. Pembroke," he stammered, straightening up into a more formal posture. Erasing from his expression a feral jealousy that he hadn't been able to control the moment he first saw Ezra at his door.

Oliver Wynn really was a very attractive man. Ezra had never been able to resist a very attractive man. He had no idea what this man's…proclivities were. But that didn't mean he couldn't look. And maneuver, if the moment was right.

"You must wonder what I'm doing here."

"Does Anna…" Oliver dropped his head a moment. "Does Her Grace need me? Is she well?"

"Calm yourself," Ezra said softly at Oliver's genuine reaction of concern. "She is very well. She requests your presence at supper."

Oliver's eyes went wide. Dark eyes, warm brown eyes. "What?" he gasped out.

"You heard me," Ezra said mildly, leaning against the doorjamb and watching as Oliver paced away.

He pivoted back and now he looked suspicious. Guarded. "Why?"

Ezra tilted his head and held the other man's gaze evenly. "I think you know why. Or do you pretend you don't?"

Oliver's jaw when tight and his eyes flashed with angry emotion. "Don't be vulgar."

"Anything but," Ezra said with a small smile. So he had not misread the situation. Good. He leaned closer, marking how Oliver's pupils dilated slightly. Interest, even against his own will. "Come join us, Mr. Wynn. Please."

Oliver let out a shaky breath and then jerked out an unsteady nod. "If that is her wish."

Ezra gave him swift directions to the dining room and smiled. "I'll join you momentarily."

Then he turned and left, his body all but humming with possibility. And a pulsing desire that felt so damned good because it had been so very long since he'd last let himself feel it.

Anna

Anna was trembling. She had no idea why, but the crackle in the air since her arrival at Mr. Pembroke's home felt both exciting and...well, dangerous. Perhaps it was because of that moment with Oliver in her bedchamber. For almost a year, she had held the man at arm's length, trying to pretend away what she knew about him. What she felt when she was near him.

She should have continued to do so, if she was trying to be fair to both of them. She should have asked Mr. Pembroke for a servant to assist her when she changed. But truth be told, she'd wanted Oliver's hands on her, even briefly. She'd wanted his breath on her neck. And God, but she wanted it still. Him still. Always.

And then there was Mr. Pembroke, himself. Ezra—he'd said his given name was when he'd loomed over her in the foyer, filling all the space and making her feel...fluttery. There was no mistaking the heat of his stare. He did nothing to hide it. But it didn't feel salacious or frightening. When he looked at her, she felt...wanted.

It was so disconcerting. All of it. Was she a wanton?

The door to the room opened and Oliver stepped in. All her thoughts faded as she stared up at him, he looked down at her... and the world seemed to slow. Spiral into focus between them.

"Oliver," she whispered.

When she said his name, he jolted and then shook his head. "I don't belong here."

She pushed to her feet and marked the way he sucked in a breath as she moved toward him. The way he never looked away from her face. The way he wavered like he wanted to lean into her. Bend into her. What would happen if he did?

His presence was at once disconcerting and comforting, but she had no intention of sending him away. Instead she reached out and took his hand. She was wearing no gloves, neither was he.

His skin was rough and warm, and God, how she wanted to feel those hands all over her.

"I need you here," she whispered. "Please."

"I'm a servant," he said, his voice shaking. "Your servant."

"Not for much longer," she said. "We both know *he'll* take you from me once I get where I'm going. This is all we have left."

There was no need to clarify that she meant the new Duke of Sedgewick when she said *he*. Oliver's jaw set, anger and pain in a potent mix that matched her own. His eyes fluttered shut and he tightened his hand against hers. "If you need me, you know I'll be here."

She nodded. "You always have been."

He opened his eyes and edged a little closer. Just a fraction closer than that and she would be in his arms. The tension that had bubbled between them in the bedchamber returned, perhaps even stronger now because they couldn't pretend it away. Their proximity wasn't because of some duty she had asked him to perform. He was near her because he wanted to be. Because she needed him like she needed breath.

"Oh good, you found your way," Ezra said as he entered the room.

Anna gasped out a breath as she pivoted away from Oliver and moved back toward her place at the table. A servant entered and laid another plate for Oliver, and Ezra motioned them to sit. They all did so, and Anna shifted as she realized she was between the men, their individual presences powerful and so very different.

There was some hustle and bustle as Ezra's staff brought out the first course and poured drinks for all. At last, the three of them were alone again.

There was a rather uncomfortable silence as they each began to eat. As if no one really knew how to proceed. Anna sighed and fell into her role as hostess, even though this wasn't her home. "Tell us about yourself, Mr. Pembroke."

Pembroke lifted his gaze and snagged her with it. She faltered with her spoon halfway to her mouth. Those really were the most remarkable eyes. Such a bright blue that they almost shone in the candlelight. So focused and intense that she felt speared into her place by him.

"What do you want to know?" he asked, his tone low.

Anna glanced toward Oliver and found him staring at her, waiting just as their host was, for her to guide the conversation. She forced a smile. "Well, you said you were the grandson of the Earl of Barrowfield, but as I thought about you, I realized you have not been much in Society these last few years."

Pembroke arched a brow and leaned back a little, a tiny smirk tilting the corner of his lips. "I'm vastly flattered by the idea you were thinking about me, Your Grace."

At that Oliver set his spoon down and made a soft noise in his throat. Almost a tiny growl, and Anna jerked her face toward him. He looked positively...untamed. Like he was only just controlling his emotions as he gripped his fists on the tabletop. She had never seen him like this before and she was shocked how arousing it was to her.

Pembroke was also watching him and inclined his head. "I beg your pardon, Your Grace. I suppose my time away from polite company has made me a bit more forward than Mr. Wynn would like."

Oliver's cheek twitched, but he didn't respond. He just continued to stare at Pembroke like he would tear him apart if he moved wrong. If he threatened Anna. She reached out and gently covered Oliver's hand with her own.

"Please," she said softly.

Oliver's fingers fluttered beneath hers and he glanced down at her hand over his. His cheeks flamed red for a moment and then he nodded. "Forgive me." He cleared his throat and looked at Pembroke. "Forgive me."

"Nothing to forgive, you fascinating creature," Pembroke said with another half-smile. "As for the question, Your Grace, you are correct. I had a…break with my family a few years ago." There was brief pain to his expression. "A break with the world, really. And I retreated here to my estate and to the places in London where a man who wants to disappear might go."

"I'm sorry," Anna said gently, and meant it.

His expression softened slightly, but he shrugged. "You needn't be. After all, it led to positive things in the end. It had to or else it would be too horrible to endure. So I worked."

"Worked?" Anna asked. "What kind of work?"

There was a brief pause as the servants brought the next course of supper. When they had departed, Pembroke tilted his head. "Painting, Your Grace. I am a painter."

Her lips parted in surprise, and beside her Oliver said, "That's why there was paint on your forearm when we arrived."

"I'm equally flattered by your attention…*Oliver*," Pembroke said.

Oliver shifted in his seat and Anna observed him closely, watching for the flare of anger again that might need to be eased. Only this time, he didn't appear angry. No, there was something else that had lit up in his gaze. Something…heated. And she swallowed hard at the unexpected sight of it. It seemed Ezra Pembroke could affect them both in ways that were entirely unpredictable.

"What—what do you paint?" she stammered, trying to gain a little purchase on the situation.

"It started with landscapes," Pembroke said. "And regular portraits. When it was a hobby, my father supported it. But once I expressed interest in selling my work, in getting out from under his thumb…well, then it became common. But I refused to stop. To bend to him."

Oliver leaned forward. "What did he do?"

"Cut me off," Pembroke admitted. "And though at first the idea was terrifying, ultimately, it allowed me a freedom I never could have imagined. It allowed me to turn to more interesting…and lucrative…subjects."

There was something hypnotic about the way he said that. Something that felt raw. Anna fought to find her breath. "What kind of subjects?" she whispered.

"Erotic portraits, Your Grace," Pembroke said simply.

Anna and Oliver both sucked in their breath at the same time, and somehow it was comforting that he was as shocked as she was by Pembroke's statement. Pembroke was watching them both now, gauging their reactions, she thought. Waiting for whatever would come next.

"I...don't understand," Anna said.

"The words or the concept?" Pembroke teased gently.

"The concept." Oliver surprised her by answering in her stead. "I think both of us are having trouble grasping the meaning."

Pembroke nodded slowly and then said, "Finish your supper and I'll show you both *exactly* what I mean."

CHAPTER 3

Oliver

It wasn't often that Oliver got to partake in a fine supper like the one that had just finished, but every bite had been like sand on his tongue as he waited for the moment when Pembroke would show them what he meant by erotic art. As much as his protective instincts...and jealousy...flared every time the man looked at Anna like she was dessert, his interest was also raised. After all, Pembroke was uncommonly attractive, and Oliver had always known what he was.

Anna held his heart, and he wanted her with a desperation that sometimes kept him up at night. But he was no monk, and he had always been attracted to both men and women. Taken his pleasure with both over the years.

But Pembroke, like Anna, was not within his reach. So he steadied himself as best he could and smiled up at the servant who had taken his plate. Supper was over now. Judging from how Pembroke was shifting, he was just as anxious about what would happen next as Oliver was. And Anna was practically coming out of her skin. Oliver knew her tells. Knew the way her breath caught when she was aroused, knew the way her pupils dilated.

He knew a great deal more than that.

"I think we've dallied long enough," Pembroke said, rising. "Oliver, why don't you escort Her Grace?"

It wasn't that Oliver hadn't done as men above his station had required for most of his life. They snapped orders, they demanded obedience and subservience from those of his class. But there was something about the way Pembroke said his words...drawled them, something about the way he said *Oliver*...and Oliver wanted to do anything the man said. Everything.

He blinked and rose to his feet, holding out a trembling arm toward Anna. "Your Grace?" he said softly.

She folded her fingers into the crook of his arm without hesitation and looked up at him, dark blue eyes soft and filled with desire. God, all that desire. He would have trembled with it except he used all his control not to.

"Follow me," Pembroke said, and exited the dining room. He led them through the twisting halls of the estate back into what seemed to be a private area away from the main rooms where guests might congregate. At a door, Pembroke took a deep breath and opened it, motioning them inside. Into a room unlike anything Oliver had ever seen, and he knew in that moment that everything was about to change.

Ezra

Normally Ezra was confident. It was a skill he'd cultivated over many years in order to combat the intense verbal berating he'd suffered from his family. He could convince himself under normal circumstances that he didn't care what anyone thought.

But as the Duchess of Pembroke and Oliver Wynn entered his studio space, he could hardly breathe from anxiety over what they might think of it all. In truth, aside from clients, who only saw the images he painted for them, no one had ever seen his private work laid out like it was in this moment.

He watched them both, saw how the duchess's mouth went slack, how Oliver's dark eyes went wide as they darted from wall to wall. They moved together toward the first painting nearest the door and walked around the entire perimeter of the space, looking at each piece like this was the most interesting museum.

He knew what they saw. These were intimate images, capturing deeply personal moments. Sexual situations between passionate partners. Some of them were traditional, men and women together. But there were also portraits that depicted two women enjoying each other, and two men. As well as all permutations that could be combined between them. People taking pleasure. That was what his work was about.

He held his breath as the duchess slid her hand away from Oliver, her cheeks bright with a blush. But she didn't seem uncomfortable as she breathed, "They are beautiful, Mr. Pembroke."

"Thank you," Ezra said softly, and speared her companion with his stare. "And what do you think, Oliver?"

Oliver stared at him, almost defiant in the way his chin lifted. There was no hiding his arousal at the situation they were in. His hard cock was outlined against the front of his trousers and Ezra's mouth practically watered at the sight of it. Wanted more.

As if the duchess sensed that tension rising in the air, she murmured, "So people come here to this studio to…to do this?" she asked. "Pose? Or do you create their images purely from your mind?"

Ezra flinched and the heat that hung between the three of them dissipated slightly. He bent his head. "Once I could find my muse without a subject, or paint from my own experiences. But in the last five years, that has changed. So yes, they come here, asking me to create something that is for their private pleasure. They trust me to look at them in these situations and to make that beautiful, not rude or salacious."

"You do a good job," Oliver said softly.

"What changed five years ago?" the duchess pressed.

Ezra cocked his head, focusing entirely on her. She was truly lovely. There was both a sweetness to her expression and an erotic knowledge that made him want to paint her. To capture that dichotomy as best he could. To capture the heat that was woven between her and her servant.

"I lost my creative drive, I suppose. For reasons I'd rather not discuss," Ezra said. "But tonight, when you two arrived at my door, I was instantly struck by something I haven't felt in a very long time. A drive to create. To make something beautiful for nothing but my own pleasure."

Oliver's nostrils flared and he edged slightly in front of the duchess. A protective move. "What are you saying?"

Ezra stepped toward him, closer and closer, until their chests were almost touching. "I want to paint Her Grace...I want to paint her with you. Like this."

~

Anna

Anna couldn't breathe, she couldn't even recall how as she stared at Pembroke, trying to understand if she was dreaming or if this was really happening. Had this man, this handsome man, suggested that she pose for an erotic portrait...with Oliver? To tangle herself with him while Pembroke watched?

And why did that arouse her to a level she hadn't allowed herself to feel in a very long time?

"How dare you?" Oliver said, his voice rough and low as he

eased himself in front of her even further, a physical wall between her and Pembroke.

Pembroke cocked his head, and Anna hoped he could see that Oliver's rage was not something to be trifled with. He practically vibrated with indignant anger and protective wrath. This was not something she'd seen before. He was, after all, a servant, and had to control his responses to his "betters". She reached out to draw her fingers into the crook of his elbow.

"Oliver," she said softly.

Perhaps under normal circumstances, that would have drawn his attention back to her. Broken the intense connection between him and Pembroke. Only Pembroke did not seem to see the danger. Or he saw it and didn't care enough to protect himself. To stand down so he wouldn't escalate this situation.

No, instead, Pembroke moved forward, eyes locked on Oliver's, a swagger to his hips. One step after another, a slow challenge that lifted the tension in the room. The heat.

Anna gasped out a breath and moved to wedge herself between the men. She reached behind her to press a hand to Oliver's chest, holding him back, even as she stared up at Pembroke. "Please!"

Pembroke stopped coming toward her. "Let me see if I can give this situation more clarity. You are running, Your Grace. That is why you were out in the middle of an ice storm in the dark."

Anna nearly choked at that simple statement that stripped her down to her very core.

"You don't have to tell me from what. To what," Pembroke continued. "But I would assume it has to do with funds. That money is why you look so desperate, why *he* looks so haunted." He paused, as if waiting for one of them to deny his charge. Of course, neither of them could. "I would pay you for posing."

Anna froze. That he could see though her, that it was humiliating, didn't change the fact that he was also correct. And that his simple statement was like a buoy to cling to in a tossing sea.

"How—how much?" she whispered, hating that her voice broke. That she couldn't sound nonchalant and unmoved like Pembroke did. Like men always did when they held enormous power.

"Fifty pounds," Pembroke said casually, as if he had not listed a number that could change the fortune of some people. His gaze flitted to Oliver. "Each."

Anna's knees began to tremble and she stumbled back. She might have fallen if Oliver hadn't caught her elbow, keeping her upright as she leaned against him. Blood whooshed in her ears, a steady throb of her own pulse making anything else hard to hear.

"Oliver," she murmured, lifting her gaze to his. He stared back, so solid, so comforting. And his expression was guarded. She fought once more for breath and for words. "I could…I could let a place for a while with that kind of money. And then perhaps I could beg friends for help. For a position even."

Oliver's cheek twitched, his pain at the idea of her having to beg for her life obvious. Of course, if she didn't, if she couldn't, then she'd have to do far worse than beg. And to a man who would rather like to see her prostrate before him. She had no one else, after all. Her family was all dead, and the new Duke of Sedgewick held so much over her head. He had already implied he would ruin any match she tried to make for a new marriage. Because he wanted her to dance to his tune.

"You wouldn't have to go to Sedgewick," Oliver said softly.

Pembroke sucked in a breath, but Anna didn't look at him. She remained focused on Oliver instead. Her island, her rock, her protector.

"It isn't fair for me to ask you," she murmured.

"You aren't," Pembroke said. "I am."

Both of them looked at him, his expression so benign for a man who was requesting something so tempting and so filled with the potential to destroy all at once.

"You needn't decide this moment," Pembroke said gently. "This weather won't let up—I would wager you'll spend another night here. Think about it, Your Grace."

Anna nodded, her head spinning with all the thoughts. Chief of which was the idea of surrendering to Oliver. Of having him in the bright lights of this studio, of surrendering to a desire that she had denied for a long time.

And of Pembroke watching while it unfolded.

"I...I need to lie down. Forgive me," she whispered, and staggered from the room, her mind wild with images of Oliver's hands on her, his mouth on her, of Pembroke's hands and mouth too.

And how impossible a fantasy it all was, even if it was being offered to her on a silver platter.

CHAPTER 4

Oliver

The moment Anna staggered from Pembroke's studio, Oliver pivoted toward the man. "What the hell do you think you're doing?" he snapped, his breath rolling from his lungs in hard pants as he stared at the man who had suggested he live out his every dream.

Pembroke shrugged. "I saw you two together. From the moment you drew her from the carriage, your desire for each other was plain. And in her bedchamber..."

Oliver shook his head. "You were spying on us?"

"I could hear breathless whispers," Pembroke said mildly. "I'm not a fool. I know you're positively feral at the idea that I want her, as well."

"Fuck you," Oliver growled, and immediately wished he could take it back. Anna wasn't his, much as he wished that were true. And he was still a servant. He could be put out on his arse for talking to this man like that and then where would he be? Where would she be?

But Pembroke only chuckled. "That's somewhat of the idea," he all but purred.

Oliver faltered at the easy suggestion. At the fact that he could see this man meant it. Pembroke wanted Anna. And Pembroke wanted him. He swallowed hard and tried to gather himself in some way. "You...you can't toy with Anna," he said. "She's had enough of that. She's been hurt enough."

Pembroke's harder stare softened slightly and he shook his head. "I assure you, I have no desire to hurt Her Grace. *Anna*."

Oliver caught his breath. He had referred to her by her first name, giving it over to Pembroke. Now the way the other man said it seemed to tingle up Oliver's spine. Made everything feel thick and heavy.

"I don't want to hurt you either," Pembroke continued. "I'm offering a solution that could be good for all of us. You two can explore the heat that is between you. I can set free the creativity my returned muse has inspired. And in the end, she'll be able to protect herself, at least for a while, from whatever danger you two don't want to share."

Oliver bent his head. He didn't trust this man enough to disclose those troubles. Even if he did, they weren't his to reveal. They were hers. He would protect them, as he wanted to protect her, until his breath ran out. He turned away and Pembroke sighed.

"Just as I said to Her Grace, I encourage you to think about what you want, Oliver." Pembroke stepped closer, invading Oliver's personal space just a fraction. He smelled good, like rain in the woods. "*Whatever* you want."

With that, Pembroke left the room and Oliver stood there, squeezing his eyes shut. What he wanted. Did he even know what that was? Well, he *did*. But he'd spent a long time suppressing every want. Servants didn't get to have those, not often.

He let out the breath in his lungs shakily and opened his eyes again. His gaze was drawn once more to the images that hung on Pembroke's studio walls. Beautiful images, but intensely erotic. He stepped closer to the one nearest him. A man and a woman's legs and arms locked, her head thrown back and mouth open with pleasure, the man's mouth buried against her breast as she rode him.

He couldn't help but picture Anna just like that. With him. Finally with him. Just the brief moment of imagining made him hard as steel and he cleared his throat. This was a dangerous suggestion and he knew it.

But he also felt so drawn to it.

He left the room and made his way upstairs. He found Anna's chamber and hesitated there, staring at the barrier between that separated him from her. He should walk away. Be the one to refuse this ridiculous suggestion and save them both from the ramifications of it.

But he didn't. He knocked. There was the sound of soft shuffling from the other side and then she opened the door. She was still in her gown but had taken her hair down. He caught his breath at the sight of her like this with brown curls tangled around her shoulders.

Her cheeks were flushed, her pupils dilated and dilating further as she stared up at him, silent.

Then she moved closer. Without a word, she pressed her hand to his chest, sliding it up, up over his shoulder, cupping his cheek. Her breath caught as she lifted up on her tiptoes, her trembling lips reaching for him.

And he forgot everything else in the world and kissed her.

Anna

Anna moaned against Oliver's tongue as their kiss deepened, grew wilder. She leaned up into him, gasping as his arms came around her, as he pushed her into the room, kicking the door shut behind them. He pivoted her, pressing her back against the barrier and leaning against her, letting her feel his weight, his warmth. His passion. Oh, yes, she felt his passion. As powerful and sharp as her own when it bloomed and spread throughout her entire body.

And she could have this. Have this man, have this pleasure, have everything…if she said yes to Pembroke's wicked suggestion. She pulled back reluctantly, still tasting Oliver on her lips even when she moved from his arms. He didn't follow her as she paced away, around to the other side of the bed, as if the barrier would make her forget what he felt like when he touched her.

"Do you want this?" Oliver asked, his voice low and rough. Intoxicating. God, how that voice moved her.

She fought for purchase on her wild emotions. "I-I don't know. All I can wonder is if it's fair to you."

He stared at her for a long moment, and something shifted in his expression. There was no longer only naked desire on his face, but something deeper and richer. Something she feared as she saw it and also wished she could have.

"You know I would do anything for you, Anna," he said, his lips trembling. "That I would pull down the stars if you asked. And if we do this, I promise you, I will live on the memory of every moment until the day I die."

Anna's heart beat faster at the passion with which he said those words, at the way he said her name, like it was some benediction that rolled off his tongue. She never wanted him to call her *Your Grace* ever again, only her name. Whispered, shouted, moaned. She'd never loved the sound of it more.

"It wouldn't be forever," she said, almost to herself as much as him. "The time here would be a bubble, something trapped behind glass that we can't reach after it's over."

He blinked. "I know that's how it would have to be."

She bent her head, her breath coming short, her hands shaking. "I want you," she murmured. "I...I want this."

She heard the rumble from deep within his chest and looked up to see his expression lined with relief. He nodded. "Then we should tell him," he said. "Though we could wait until tomorrow, to see if you change your mind."

Anna shook her head and came back around the bed. She took his hand and lifted it, pressing a kiss to his rough knuckles, lifting his fingers to lean her cheek into their weight. He clenched them against her skin gently, his lips parting.

"I'm not going to change my mind, Oliver. And I don't want to waste whatever time we have here." She held his gaze, lost in him, lost in the surprise and delight of what was going to happen. "Let's tell him now."

～

Ezra

Ezra was in his chamber, half-undressed, when there was a light knock on his door. He glanced toward the sound, wrinkling his brow. He had asked not to be disturbed—he wanted to think about all that had happened in such a short span of time.

He moved to the door and opened it to find Oliver and Anna standing there. Together. As always, Oliver was slightly in front of her, a partial wall of protection. One Ezra found himself desperately wanting to prove was not required.

"Oliver, Anna," he said, noting how Anna caught her breath at this, his first usage of her given name. "I didn't expect you so soon. Do you need anything?"

"We—we want to do it," Anna stammered, reaching out to take

Oliver's hand. His fingers slid between hers and he squeezed gently. A reassurance that felt as intimate as anything they would potentially do next. Ezra remembered what that kind of connection felt like.

He swallowed. "You want me to paint you. Together. The way the other pieces in my studio are done?" He needed to reiterate those facts, to be certain all parties fully understood. "You know that I'll watch you together. That I'll see everything you do to each other."

Oliver shifted, and Ezra couldn't help but notice the hard ridge of his erection pressed against his trousers. God, but that man was irresistible. How had Anna managed it all this time?

"I know," she said. "I want…I want that, too."

Ezra let his eyes shut and his breath exit his lungs in a shaky sigh. "And what about you, Oliver? Do you want me to watch you?"

When he looked at him, he found Oliver's gaze locked firmly and confidently on his. "I do, Pembroke."

"Ezra," Ezra corrected. "If we're going to do something so wicked, so lovely, so vulnerable…then I think you should call me Ezra."

Anna nodded. "Ezra," she murmured.

Ezra noted that Oliver didn't call him by his name. That was fine. In time, that might come. He motioned toward the hallway. "Then let's go to my studio. I don't want to waste a moment of this creative inspiration that you two have brought back to me. I want to paint you. Tonight."

They walked back to the studio space together in an awkward silence. As Ezra got out his pencils and a sketchpad, Oliver shifted at the doorway and Anna walked around the space, staring once more at the erotic paintings Ezra had done in the past. Ezra could see her drinking in those images, studying what he had created before. Was she imagining herself in those same scenarios with Oliver? If so, it seemed to arouse her. The edginess to her body language was clear and it seemed to be from anticipation rather than fear or regret.

"Where do you want us?" Oliver asked, his voice a little shaky.

That question pierced Ezra's fog and he glanced at him. God, all the answers to that question. But he knew what was meant and crossed the room to a filmy curtain. He drew it back and revealed a large bed.

"It's your choice. Here or the settee. In front of the fire on the rug," he said, motioning all around the room at the places one could play.

Oliver looked toward Anna, of course. The man's feelings were patently obvious. She was the focus. Always.

She looked toward the settee. "There?" she suggested softly.

Oliver nodded and moved to the couch. She followed and for a moment, they just stared at each other, tension thick between them. Tension and uncertainty.

Ezra moved closer, dragging a chair near so he could see better when they began. "I'll sketch you," he explained, hoping to make them more comfortable. "I may move a bit to get different angles. But I won't interfere." He hesitated. He so wanted to add, *unless you want me to.* This wasn't the right time for that. "There is nothing you can do wrong. This is about your pleasure. You'll simply have an audience."

Anna let out a soft laugh, though there was little humor to it, more nervousness.

Ezra tilted his head. "I understand it may be difficult, the idea of being watched while you do something so intimate, with a person you haven't had experience with before."

She looked away from Oliver at last and her dark blue eyes held his. Her cheeks brightened, but she didn't hesitate as she said, "I've been watched before, Ezra. At the Donville Masquerade. And as for Oliver..." Her hands shook and she gripped them at her sides as she returned her attention to him. "I...I know it was you that night. I know it was you in the hallway, when I was watching my husband with his mistress."

Ezra's eyes went wide. Even without full knowledge of what she spoke, the context was clear. They'd shared what had been a supposed anonymous encounter. And judging from the way all the color drained from Oliver's face in that moment, it wasn't something they'd ever discussed before.

This night had just become all the more interesting.

CHAPTER 5

Oliver

He couldn't breathe. It was impossible as Oliver stared down into Anna's face and he saw the secret that had hung between them torn into the light. In front of an alluring stranger.

"Anna," he breathed. "I…I'm sorry."

"Why?" she asked, and sounded truly baffled by his apology. "I wanted you so much that night. I needed exactly what you gave me as you held me against the wall and thought only of my pleasure. And I've dreamed of that night over and over again. I don't want you to be sorry."

He drew in a shaky breath. "When did…when did you know it was me?"

She smiled, a little sad. "That night. I knew the moment I came out of the hell with Sedgewick and you were there waiting for us. When you touched my hand, it was electric. And I thought of that stranger's whiskers against my thighs. Of his low, rough voice, and I knew instantly that it was you."

He couldn't have been more shocked by any other statement.

His heart throbbed. "I wanted to tell you. It felt wrong to keep it from you."

"I saw that. I saw it hang on your tongue so many times," she whispered.

He shook his head. "Why didn't *you* say something?"

She shrugged. "As I said to you that night when you tried to confess your identity in the hall, it was a moment meant for the dark. And it would only have complicated things." She sighed. "It complicated things enough, though I have never regretted it."

She rested her hand on his chest, just as she had in her room earlier. Her fingers clenched against the fabric of his jacket and he felt the pressure of each one as if she were gripping his heart with her bare hand. "But I want all of you now, Oliver. In the light. Without masks. I want to see your pleasure, I want to take it like you took mine that night. I want all of that. And I don't care about the cost anymore."

Oliver glanced at Ezra from the corner of his eye and found him sitting in the chair close by, pencil in a white-knuckled grip. He was sketching them already, but when he lifted his pale blue gaze, his desire was evident. Anna and Oliver had an audience, and he was part of this now. Not something Oliver ever would have guessed would arouse him just as her touch did.

And so he surrendered to it.

He caught Anna around the waist and drew her to him slowly, gently. She shivered as her curves molded to his chest and her eyes fluttered shut when she lifted her mouth in offering. He took it. Gently at first, he was always gentle with her, but hunger began to take over. Desire. The realization that he would have, even for a brief moment, this woman who he'd believed he'd never have again. Better yet, he would truly have her. He would feel the flex of her around his cock, watch her as she came instead of feeling it in the dark.

No, he couldn't think of those things. He would spend too quickly, and he wanted to savor this stolen moment. Milk it for all he could. After all, he had to believe it would truly never come again.

He pushed his hands into her hair and the soft silkiness was heaven against his fingers. She grunted and lifted against him, her body beginning to tremble as she leaned like he was her support.

"Please," she murmured against his lips.

Near them, Ezra made a soft sound in his throat and Oliver glanced toward him. Ezra was still sketching, but his pupils were widely dilated and his arousal was clear and almost as tempting as Anna's.

"Please," she repeated, tugging on Oliver's jacket and returning his full attention to her. Her gaze was lifted to his, beseeching. He nodded slowly and then he unfastened the buttons along the front of her gown. As he loosened them, he revealed more and more of the silk chemise beneath. It had lace at the top, which outlined her breasts. God, her breasts. So perfect, like they had been sized to fit his palms. He slid his hands past the fabric of her gown to test that theory.

She gasped and rubbed herself against his hands. Her nipples were hard and got harder. He was nearly washed away by it all, but he carefully centered himself and slid her gown to pool at her feet.

She was wearing just that chemise now and pretty stitched stockings. He leaned back to look at her, drinking her in, memorizing every gorgeous curve and hollow of her full figure. She was glorious. His every dream and fantasy come to life.

"Touch me, Oliver," she whimpered, grasping his hand and returning it to her breast. He stroked her nipple through the lace with his thumb, and she trembled. When he bent his head and sucked her through the fabric, she cried out and her head fell back. Her fingers came into his hair, holding him against her. He sucked harder, swirling around the tip through the lace, and she ground against him.

He continued to suck her, one nipple, then the other, even as he looped his fingers beneath the straps of her chemise. He moved away and slid the fabric down, leaving her naked but for the stockings. He stared at her. Her nipples were a dark rose, almost brown, and they were puckered with pleasure.

Next to them, Ezra gasped softly. Oliver looked at him again. He'd stood and his trembling hand hesitated over the sketchpad he still held. He was clearly enraptured by Anna—he couldn't take his eyes off of her. And Oliver was jealous. He recognized that feeling in his chest. He'd certainly felt it before when it came to the late duke, who got to have Anna's company any time he desired it and yet squandered that gift.

But he also felt something else as he watched Ezra fall under Anna's spell just as he had. Oliver felt excited. He gently turned her, giving the other man a better view of her. Of them. Then he brushed his cheek against her now bare breast.

She gripped at his shoulders at the rasp of his beard against the sensitive flesh, and he smiled. God, how he loved to please her. He would do it all his life if he could. But he couldn't. He couldn't afford to forget that, either. This was a beautiful little stolen moment, nothing more. It would never be more.

He pushed all those thoughts aside and returned his focus to her body. He glided his fingers down her sides, across the softness of her curves. Just as he had that long ago night when he pleasured her in the dark, he memorized every line of her. And now he added the look of her, too. The way she panted, the way she shifted, the gorgeous glow of her skin, the fact that she had a dark pink splotch of a birthmark along her ribcage.

He began to kiss along the under curve of her breasts and down along her side. He traced the line of her, lightly nibbling and sucking as he went to his knees at her feet. When he looked up at her, her eyes were wide and wild.

"What is it?" he asked, even as he brushed his fingers across her hip.

"I want you inside of me," she whispered, whimpered. "Not just your tongue."

He stared at her, this amazing woman who was begging for him, and he felt such a swell of possessive desire that he could have put her on her back on that settee and drilled into her in a heartbeat. But he tempered it, carefully and smiled up at her instead.

"I promise you, I want to be inside of you. But I've been dreaming of your taste for a very long time. I want that on my tongue again."

"Yes," Ezra breathed, and the scratch of his pencil increased.

Every reminder that he was witness to this moment was more and more exciting to Oliver. And he could tell by the way that Anna looked at him, it was for her, as well. Oliver pushed her legs wider. She balanced against his shoulders, as she had done that night in the hallway, tilting her hips to give him better access to her pussy.

He slid his hands up her thighs, over the garters tied neatly there. She murmured his name. She shouted it when he spread her lips and revealed the wet shine of her entrance.

"Goddamn it," Oliver muttered before he leaned up and licked her.

She tasted the same. Earthy and sweet, salty and fresh. He cupped her backside and buried his face between her legs, licking and sucking her over and over as she gripped his hair and ground against him in building pleasure. He looked up her writhing body, reveling in her flushed cheeks, her panting breaths, the thin sheen of sweat that broke out on her brow. She was so damned close and he wanted to feel her release flood his tongue like it had all those months ago.

When it happened, it was spectacular. Even better than his most vivid memories of that moment. She cried out, her body flexing against him, out of control and wild. She tugged his hair, she smashed her body into his and her knees buckled so that he had to support her with his hands to keep her upright.

Only when the flutters of her body subsided did he rise back to his feet. She cupped his cheeks instantly and kissed him, licking her essence from his lips even as her hands fumbled at his jacket.

"Slow," he groaned, because he feared if they moved too quickly he would lose all semblance of control.

She broke the kiss and shook her head. "No. I don't want you to leave again."

There was something in the way she said those words. Some pain hidden behind the arousal. He glanced back and saw that Ezra had stopped sketching. His brows were lifted. He'd heard it too.

Oliver caught her hands and lifted them to his lips. "I'm not going anywhere, Anna. Not tonight. I promise."

Her desperation faded a fraction and she drew a deep breath. "Good. But I still want to see you. All of you. Please."

The added *please* was what hit him in the gut. Said so damned sweetly even though her voice was rougher with desire.

He nodded and unbuttoned the jacket. He tossed it behind himself and went to work unbuttoning his shirt. He tugged it over his head and heard both Ezra and Anna take sharp breaths. She was staring at him, her eyes wide. She extended a soft hand and laid it against his bare chest and his heart almost stopped. She let her hand slide down, across his stomach, around to his side. It was almost as if she had no idea how much her touch moved him.

Ezra stepped forward and licked his lips. Oliver almost wished, in that charged moment, that he would join them. That he'd put his hands on Oliver, too. That both of them would touch him and hold him and they would all move together like one animal seeking pleasure.

But he didn't. Ezra shook his head like he was waking from some delicious dream and went back to sketching, his pencil moving wildly across the paper.

"Take off the rest," Anna whispered.

"Of course, Your Grace," Oliver murmured as he unfastened the buttons on his fall front and pushed the trousers away.

"Oh my God," Anna breathed, staring down at his extremely hard and very ready cock. She let her hand draw lower and wrapped her fingers around him. With just the perfect pressure, she stroked him base to head, and it took everything in him not to spend right there and then. Anna was touching him. Really touching him.

"Sit down," she said, her tone suddenly sharp and with a different kind of desperation.

He did as he'd been told, widening his legs a little as he stared up at her, waiting for her. Waiting for everything.

She pressed each hand into the back of the settee on either side of his head and then straddled his lap, sinking down over him slowly. She kissed him as she ground down, letting him feel the wetness of her before she reached between them, positioned him and took him inside of her inch by inch.

Anna

Oliver stretched Anna's body and it was delicious. Better than anything she'd ever felt before. She took him fully inside and then hesitated, just feeling him. The width, the length, the heat. She wanted to notice every bit of it, savor it. Because this was a moment she'd never thought she'd be gifted. She wanted to take full advantage now.

He made a low sound in his throat and lifted slightly, grinding against her clitoris, still sensitive from the orgasm from his talented mouth and tongue.

Anna gripped her legs against Oliver's thighs, feeling the prickle of his leg hair against her skin. Rather like when he had his face between her legs and let his stubbled cheeks rake along her in teasing strokes. She bucked against the pleasure of that thought and ground harder against him. He dug the fingers of one hand into her right hip, cupped and guided her backside with the other. His touch was warm and rough and oh, so very perfect.

Together they rose and fell, building toward the crescendo of this storm. She felt it coming, pleasure pulsing through her body, focusing between her legs at her clitoris, at the inside of her body where she gripped his hard cock almost out of her own control.

He was doing this to her, this man she had fantasized about for years. Even before she'd realized he was her shadowy lover one beautiful time at the Donville Masquerade. He was her dream, her wish, her fantasy.

And now he stared up at her as she rode him, his warm brown eyes locking with hers, holding her steady. She slowed in her strokes, her breath dissipating as he murmured, "Don't look away from me, Anna. I want to see it all."

She nodded and kept her eyes locked even as pleasure over-flowed through her. Wracking, wild pulses of release made her hips buck and her pussy clench over and over again. He held her tighter, but he never looked away. He stared at her, almost in worship as he took every thrust of her body, as he savored every rock of her hips.

It was magical, it was mystical, it was perfect beyond her dreams. Only when the shuddering strokes had faded did he lift from beneath her, dragging her mouth to his to claim her lips while he fucked her hard and fast from below. She dug her nails into his shoulders, trying to find purchase in the face of animal hunger. He drove his tongue in the same beat as his cock and then he grunted, he moaned, he cried out in the quiet of the room and pushed her from his body to come between them.

For a moment, the room was silent. Anna pressed her forehead to Oliver, matching their panting breaths until they slowed. She heard Ezra move from behind her and glanced over her shoulder at him.

He licked his lips, his arousal obvious in the cock outlined against his fawn breeches. And even though she had just experienced such pleasure, she wanted to do the same all over again. It was a strange thing, to feel so much desire, for two different men. To want something she would have been taught was wicked and not give a damn.

At least not now.

"Ezra?" she whispered.

He swallowed hard. "That was magnificent," he said, voice rough. "And I cannot wait to paint what I sketched. Now, would you two mind if I posed you? Just so I can find the position I liked most."

Anna found heat flooding her cheeks and she glanced down at Oliver. His face was still relaxed with pleasure, but he lifted his brows. "Only if you want to," he reassured her gently.

She nodded. He would protect her. Such a strange thing to know like she knew her own face in a mirror. But then, she had always known that. Oliver would do *anything* to keep her safe.

"I don't mind," she said, and she meant it. She didn't know what posing entailed, but if it meant Ezra would come closer…

Oliver looked past her to Ezra. "Do what you will."

Ezra set his sketchbook down and stepped toward them. Both she and Oliver tracked his movements. She heard Oliver's intake of breath, just like her own when Ezra stopped just next to them on the settee.

"Put your hand here," Ezra said, setting her fingers on Oliver's shoulder lightly. "And you…" He lifted Oliver's hand from his own thigh and placed it where her backside curved.

When he did so, Oliver made an animal, hungry sound deep in his throat. And Anna could take it no more. She flexed around Oliver's lap, feeling his cock stir against her once more.

"Kiss him," she whispered.

Both men froze and Oliver moved his gaze to her. "What?"

"I can see you want to," she explained. "I'm not a fool and I'm certainly not as innocent as I might appear to be. You two want each other, don't you?"

Both men were silent a moment, staring at each other. It was like she wasn't there in that moment, even though Ezra's breath was caressing her skin and Oliver's hand was cupping her backside gently. They were both caught up in each other.

Finally, instead of answering, Ezra leaned down. His fingers slid into Oliver's thick hair and he gently tilted the other man's head. Then he lowered his mouth, slowly, painfully slowly, perhaps to give Oliver a chance to pull away. But he didn't.

And they kissed.

CHAPTER 6

Oliver

Ezra Pembroke tasted like mint and a hint of whisky. He tasted like desire and forbidden fantasies that Oliver had always kept close to his chest, exploring only in places where he felt completely safe. His head spun as Ezra's tongue gently probed past his lips, as he made a low groan of pleasure that seemed to reverberate through every nerve ending in Oliver's body.

And if that wasn't enough, Anna ground down on his lap, making her own little sigh of pleasure and desire. Oliver didn't know what to do with it all. He'd been aware for a very long time that he loved Anna. He'd tried not to label it, but it had swelled so powerfully as she rode him, her eyes locked with his, that he couldn't deny it to himself anymore. He loved her, he had always loved her, he would always love her.

But now there was this other person, wedging himself into the mix. And Ezra's kiss was so fucking intoxicating, it made Oliver wish he could have everything.

At last Ezra pulled away. He smiled down at Oliver and his

fingers glided gently out of his hair. He focused his attention on Anna now. "And what about you, Your Grace?" he asked.

She wobbled against Oliver, her legs tightening around his ever so slightly. "Me?"

"Do you want a kiss, as well?" Ezra asked, his tone hypnotic.

She glanced at Oliver, looking for permission that he was not equipped to give. She wasn't his. She could never be his aside from what had just happened. Still, he found himself nodding, fascinated as Ezra cupped her chin and tilted it upwards. Her breath wobbled from her lungs as he brushed his lips to hers. Teasing, toying until Anna's fingers tightened against Oliver's shoulders. Oliver shifted, cupping her backside tighter, rubbing her against him until she moaned lightly against Ezra's lips and Ezra shuddered with pleasure.

Then he stepped back. "Stay with me," he said, his tone low and rough.

Anna blinked in what seemed to be confusion and Oliver's eyes went wide. "What does that mean?"

"You'll have to stay tomorrow anyway, thanks to the storm. But stay longer. Stay the week. Stay with me and let me paint you. Stay with me and let me...let me be with you. Both of you."

There was a flicker of vulnerability in that request. One that Ezra quickly erased from his features. But Oliver had seen it. Beneath that commanding presence was a man who longed for connection. Longed for passion. Longed for...well, perhaps all people longed for more. But when he saw that brief sparkle in this man's gorgeous blue eyes, he wanted to lean into it. To save him.

But now it was gone and the question remained.

"You want to be with us?" Anna asked softly. "Each?"

"Both," Ezra corrected softly. "Unless the idea of it troubles you."

Anna's brow arched. "You seem to be under the impression that I am an innocent little lamb. But I'm not. I have not been with two men at the same time, but..." She shivered. "The idea has always been intoxicating. And since I'm going to go into a situation with very few pleasures, I want all the pleasure I can have now. Only this isn't just my decision. Oliver has a right to refuse."

"I would do whatever you desired," Oliver said instantly.

Ezra shook his head. "Not good enough. If we are to do this, Oliver, I want it to be because you want me. You want to feel my cock inside of you. You want to watch me touch her and taste her while your cock is in her mouth. That you want to show me how to make her come as hard and as powerfully as you just did. That's the only way this works."

Oliver was shaking with the power of those words. With the images and the longing that they created. He didn't respond with words but reached up to cup the back of Ezra's neck. He drew him down and kissed him again, slow and long and deep. Then he released him and did the same to Anna, feeling her sag against him in renewed desire. Their flavors mingled on his tongue and made his head spin.

"I want all of that," he whispered, his voice trembling.

Ezra nodded and motioned to the big bed that had been hidden behind the curtain. The one Anna and Oliver had foregone for the use of the settee while they made love. "May I suggest we take this to the bed?"

Anna leaned in and kissed Oliver again, then slowly eased herself off his lap. Ezra took her hand and led her to the bed, where she climbed up and rested back against the pillows. Oliver followed and Ezra motioned at him to join her.

"I'm going to undress," he explained. "Make her come again. I want her wet for me."

"I'm wet already," Anna said with a light laugh that Oliver hadn't heard in a very long time. Clearly this surrender was good for her soul, as powerful a reason as any to fully commit to it.

"Are you going to let that challenge go unmet?" Ezra asked, arching a brow at Oliver.

"I think I must rise to the occasion," Oliver said, climbing up on the bed and crawling to her as he watched her pupils dilate with excitement. He kissed her once more, their tongues tangling wildly, then settled beside her, pushing her legs open so he could place the flat of his hand between them.

And oh yes, she was wet. So very, very wet. He spread her outer lips, gliding his fingers through the sticky heat of her, and she shuddered as she arched against him. He stroked her, not teasing her. No, the time for teasing was over. And as he circled his thumb around her clitoris, he watched Ezra undress. Oliver could still taste him on his tongue, and he licked his lips as the other man sat to remove his boots, then rose to unbutton his shirt.

Oliver added a finger to Anna's sheath, another, and she bucked, whimpering her pleasure. He turned his attention to her flushed face, reveling in the way she whispered his name as she began to flutter with another orgasm. She arched against his hand, moaning and thrusting her hips against him as she came. Her gaze moved past him as she did so and her eyes went wide.

She drew Oliver to kiss her, then turned his face gently so he was looking again at Ezra. While Oliver pleasured Anna, the other man had made quick work of the remainder of his clothing and stood naked at the foot of the bed, watching them as he stroked himself.

"Look at him," Anna breathed. "Look at how beautiful he is."

Oliver couldn't look away, even if he tried. He stared at Ezra, at the lean muscle that was highlighted across his broad shoulders, down his flat stomach, his toned thighs. And then there was his cock. A mouthwatering cock that Oliver wanted to touch so much it almost physically hurt.

"He is very beautiful," he agreed, close to her ear.

"What would you do to him?" Anna asked, her voice trembling with excitement.

Oliver swallowed and met Ezra's bright eyes. "I would put him in my mouth. I would make him so hard for you, Anna."

Ezra made a soft sound in his throat, something hungry and

animal and filled with desire. He stepped toward the bed, toward Oliver, and stopped touching himself. Oliver filled the gap, reaching for him, taking him in hand. He was hard as steel, but the skin along his cock was so fucking soft that Oliver worried his rough hands wouldn't be good enough. It seemed it wasn't a problem, though, because Ezra rocked against his palm, forcing a long, heavy stroke as he stared down at him.

Oliver did as he had suggested he would and leaned in, swirling his tongue around the tip of the other man. He sucked him deep into his throat, then back out, and somehow Ezra became impossibly harder.

Anna was moaning now, arching against his side as she watched them. She said nothing, just glided herself over him, straddling his lap a second time. She took him inside of her and he grunted at the pleasure, magnified by what he was doing with his mouth.

Ezra began to fuck his throat, gently at first, but harder when it became clear that Oliver could bear it. That he liked it. And God, how he liked it. There was nothing like it, knowing he was bringing this man pleasure. Watching as Ezra gripped his hands against the edge of the bed and got closer and closer to the edge.

He was close to spending, Oliver could tell that, and the way Anna's thrusts had become more erratic, it seemed she was close to another orgasm, as well. Oliver drew Ezra from his mouth and stared up at him. "I can tell you she is very wet and ready for you. If you still want her."

Ezra made a low, animal sound in his chest and caught Anna from under the arms. He bent and kissed her, rough and wild, as he drew her from Oliver's lap and set her down on the floor next to the bed. He faced her away from him, bending her over the high edge. She rested her hands on Oliver's stomach for purchase as Ezra speared her with his cock. Oliver leaned over to reach between her legs, stroking her clitoris, and she cried out, her body convulsing with the orgasm she'd been close to when she rode Oliver.

"Bloody hell," Ezra grunted, gripping her shoulders as he took her hard and fast. As Anna sagged against the bed, grinding against Ezra as her orgasm faded, Oliver gripped his own cock, stroking in time to Ezra's strokes, lost in what he saw and felt and how gorgeous this moment was. And how he never wanted it to end.

Anna

Anna felt like she was flying as Ezra took her, out of control and hungry. His cock felt so good inside of her, as her sheath fluttered from orgasm after orgasm at the hands and mouths and cocks of these remarkable men. She looked at Oliver, watching as he stroked himself. She and Ezra were his erotic show and she ground back harder, arching her back so that he could enjoy it all even more.

He was gasping, as was Ezra, both men on the brink of control. Would they come together? How much that idea aroused her even further and Ezra gasped, "God, you are so wet."

He wasn't wrong. She'd never been quite so wet. Not when she touched herself, not when touched by another man, except for perhaps the hallway encounter with Oliver all those many months ago.

"God, I want to spend in you," Ezra moaned. "But…" He withdrew and she felt the hot splash of come against her back. The sight of it seemed to push Oliver over the edge and he, too, cried out, long spurts of come splashing from his cock against his fingers.

Then he leaned forward and kissed her. Slower now, deeper, a lazy expression of satisfaction. She smiled against his mouth before he pulled away. Then Ezra turned her, leaning her back on the bed, her head resting against Oliver's hip as Ezra kissed her, too. Oliver smoothed his fingers through her hair as he did so and she was brought back to life once more. Shockingly, powerfully.

But both men seemed spent, and Ezra lifted his head and smiled at Oliver. "Now, this bed is fine and good," he said. "But mine is better. Shall we retire there? For sleep. And maybe more?"

Oliver nodded and so did Anna. She was suddenly exhausted from the stress of what had brought her here and then the absolute pleasure she had so unexpected found instead.

And the idea that she would sleep tucked between these two men, sheltered and safe, was wonderful. Even if it was only temporary.

CHAPTER 7

Anna

Anna opened her eyes, and for a moment she was entirely confused. Where was she? What was this big, beautiful chamber where muted winter light streamed through the windows?

And then it rushed back: the dangerous ride through the icy rain, the pleasures she'd shared with Ezra and Oliver. And falling asleep with both men at her sides, their hands sliding along her skin until she drifted into dreams.

But as she looked around, she realized both of them weren't in the bed now. Oliver was there, sprawled on his stomach beside her, covers low on his hips, revealing the muscled plains of his back. He was lightly snoring and she smiled. She would let him sleep—he had more than earned it, and not just the previous night.

But Ezra was nowhere to be found.

She leaned over and pressed a kiss to one of Oliver's shoulders. He made a soft sound of pleasure but didn't wake. She was careful not to wake him as she got up, either.

Her dress was in a pile on the floor, but she didn't want to take all the time to don that, so instead she grabbed for a silk robe that was draped on the back of a chair. It had to have been Ezra's because it was leagues too large for her. Still, she tied the long sash and slipped from the room, padding barefoot through the quiet house. Ezra didn't appear to be upstairs, so she crept down. There had to be servants in this big, rambling estate, but she didn't see or hear them. A blessing since she wasn't ready for them to see her sneaking around in their employer's robe, her hair tangled from sin.

She saw the door to the studio slightly cracked and went to it, drawing a deep breath before she opened it and looked inside.

Ezra stood before a canvas by the window, light haloing him like some kind of glorious fallen angel. He hadn't seemed to notice her entry, for he was entirely focused on his work. He didn't wear a shirt and the muscles in his arms stretched and contracted as he slashed brush strokes across the canvas with confidence. Occasionally he paused, drawing a deep breath and tapping his mouth with the handle of the brush as he tilted his head in intense scrutiny of his own work.

"Ezra," she said softly.

He jumped a little at the sound of her voice and looked up at her. "Anna, I didn't hear you."

"No, you seemed very focused," she said. "I'm sorry to interrupt you."

He set the brush down and shook his head. "Not at all. Were you having trouble sleeping? It's very early and we were up late."

She blushed a little at the memory of what had kept them all up so late. He smiled, like her expression gave away so much that pleased him.

"I'll admit, when I woke and you weren't there, I worried," she said, stepping farther into the room.

He tracked her every movement and suddenly his expression

was a little darker. A little more intense. "Hmmm. But Oliver was there."

She nodded. "Yes. But sound asleep, and I did not wish to wake him. He would never say it, but I know he was exhausted by yesterday. Having to drive in such weather, worrying about me. Between that and the amazing things we all shared, I think no one deserves rest more."

Ezra inclined his head. "That is likely true. He does not easily shed the role of servant. Even when he is between your legs."

Anna swallowed. She knew that was true. Oliver might give her pleasure, protection, care…all that she could desire. But he would also always hold himself just a little away. Never let her give as much as she took. Did it trouble her? More now than ever before.

She shrugged the thoughts away. "May I see the painting?"

He smiled, broader this time, and she caught her breath. The man had only smirked and tempted and teased his smile until now. But this…this was something else. He looked younger, warmer, when he truly smiled. And she wanted him as she stood there in this space that was so very much his.

"Not yet," he said and motioned to a seat by the fire. "But you can keep me company if you don't wish to return to bed."

She did so, tucking her legs beneath her, smoothing his robe so she wouldn't be too revealing. Not that the man hadn't seen her naked and spread out already. She gripped the arms of the chair at the memory.

He returned to his painting. Back to those confident brush-strokes. Her gaze shifted to the paintings around her, the ones that she could see.

"You are very talented," she said.

He didn't lift eyes from his work, but he smiled a little again. "As are you, Your Grace."

"Please don't call me that," she said, and immediately wished she could take it back when her voice broke. She felt so vulnerable. Even more so when he paused in his painting and lifted his icy blue eyes to hers. He held there and then slowly inclined his head.

"My apologies, Anna," he said. "I used the term playfully, but I know that there can be complicated feelings about a title. And I've guessed that your marriage might not have been the happiest. I won't do it again."

She drew in a breath at that response. How many times had she asked for what she wanted or needed in her life, only to be met by resistance or indignation or even cruelty? This apology and earnest promise not to cause her pain again was so refreshing. So attractive.

"Thank you," she said softly.

He lowered his gaze to the piece. "I'd actually like to know more about you."

She stiffened. "Wh-Why?"

"Because what happened between us was…unexpected."

"Oh," she said, surprised by that statement. "I would have thought a man like you would have indulged in such pleasures with the subjects of his paintings many times."

He chuckled a little. "I have, yes. But that was usually after weeks of flirting as I discussed the project with them. I knew the encounters were likely to happen before the carriages pulled up to my door."

"And Oliver and I stumbled into your life with no preamble," she said. "I see."

"Don't mistake me," he said, dabbing his brush into the paint and tapping it against the canvas gently. "The desire I feel for you is very welcome, but it wasn't what I thought I'd be experiencing twenty-four hours ago when I was reading in my study, innocent as a lamb."

She snorted out a laugh and it made him smile at her again. "I don't think you have ever been innocent as a lamb, Ezra. I have that sense."

"Hmmm. Well, either way, I'd like to know more about the woman who has inspired this passion in me and in Oliver. As well as the burst of creativity that has been painting for myself, rather than merely as a commission."

She shifted. "I admit, the idea that I inspire passion or creativity or anything at all is a rather foreign concept. My husband didn't seem to think any of those things."

His brow furrowed but he didn't look up. She thought it was to allow her some privacy with her reaction, her feelings. She appreciated that.

"Then he was a fool," he said softly, but there was a dangerous edge to his voice. "I remember him a little, actually. And I'm certain that assessment is accurate."

She found herself smiling a little now at his gentle championing. "Well, he is a dead fool now." She sighed. "It was an arranged marriage, of course. That is the way of our world usually. I wanted to make it work—I hoped for something more to come of it. But he was not interested in loving his wife, not when he could love any other woman who crossed his path and winked at him." She heard the bitterness in her voice and cleared her throat. "By the time he died, we were strangers. He didn't even stay in the house anymore. He hardly ever said my name."

Ezra looked up. "I'm sorry, Anna. Was it hurtful?"

"At first, of course." She shook her head. "I was innocent when we married. I had told myself fairytale stories. But as the years went by, that pain faded a great deal. I began to take pleasure in what independence existed. And what friendships could be made."

"Friendships," Ezra repeated, and the way he drew the word out made her know he, too, was thinking of Oliver. "You're talking about him."

Him. There was only one him. Only had been for so very long. She nodded. "Yes. Oliver." She lifted her gaze to Ezra's. "I always liked him. I won't deny it."

"How could you not?" Ezra said with a little shiver. "That face. That voice."

She shivered, too. "It does rumble through you, doesn't it? But it was more than that. He has always been so kind to me, whether he was helping me into a carriage or...or whether he found me weeping over what should have been."

Ezra swallowed. "I see."

"Nothing happened," she hastened to add, as if she were protecting Oliver's reputation. "He was comforting. Gentle. We talked. It only drew me closer to him. Once my husband died and the funds began to dry up, the servants began to quit. But never Oliver. He took the reduced salary without a word and even took over a great many duties that had been abandoned. He organized my household and invitations. He became so much more than my driver."

"Your friend," Ezra said.

She nodded. "And of course, I must repeat that he is so very handsome."

"He is that," Ezra said, rough. It made her think of his expression when Oliver had been sucking him. It was rather comforting, actually, to be able to share that attraction to someone who understood.

"It seems at least once, though, he was more than your friend. You mentioned the Donville Masquerade last night."

She sighed. She'd thought this subject might come up at some point. But there was no use hiding now, not with a man who had already been so intimately involved with them both.

"My husband used to take me there every week," she explained. "He said it was for us, but it wasn't. Ultimately, I did take lovers. But none were like the person I thought was a stranger in a dark hallway one night."

When Ezra shifted with desire, she quickly recounted that heady night. At the end, she shrugged. "I probably always knew it was him," she finished. "His voice...the voice is so recognizable.

That rough timber, the tone of it, the way it draws you closer? It's very…him. But I wanted to pretend. And once I fully realized that it was Oliver, what could I do? To reveal the truth would threaten both our futures. So I left it alone and so did he. Until it was safe."

Ezra smiled. "I'm glad that you felt safe here."

"I did," she said. "But I also know that…our relationship will soon change. He can't remain my servant for long."

She pursed her mouth as Ezra pierced her with a sharp look. She really didn't want to talk about the horrors that might still come. The dangers. No one could save her, not in the long run, she didn't think. She didn't want that horrible future to come to ruin the present.

She got up and moved toward him, watching his pupils dilate as she did so. He wanted her, even though he'd already had her. Amazing. She'd for so long convinced herself that no man could. Now there were two who did.

"May I ask you a question?"

His eyebrows lifted. She could tell he wanted to push the subject of her future, but didn't. "Of course."

"How did you know you were attracted to both women and men?"

He shook his head. "I just did. Always. I think pleasure is meant to be sought, and I find it a great deal of places. Does that bother you?"

His expression betrayed how much her answer meant and she didn't intend to withhold it for long. But before she could say anything, she heard Oliver's voice behind her, "I'm very interested in that answer, as well."

She turned to find him standing in the doorway. Unlike them, he was fully dressed, back in the plain garb he wore as her servant. But he wasn't looking at her like he was hers to command. In that moment there was a possessive hunger on his face. And she couldn't wait to see where it led.

~

Ezra

Ezra couldn't breathe as he stared at Oliver, standing in his studio door. The fact that he and Anna were in various states of undress and the other man was fully clothed somehow added to the charged element in the room. They could be at his mercy if he could just let go of his fear of crossing the line.

What would that be like?

Anna cleared her throat, and his attention was returned to her and the answer she had been about to give. He thought he already knew it, but he wanted to hear it. He thought Oliver *needed* to.

"I like seeing you together." She stepped toward Ezra again, closer. He moved around from behind the canvas where he'd been painting and she slid up beside him, pushing her body against his. Together they looked at Oliver.

Oliver shifted at the door, swallowing hard. Ezra supposed that was what she wanted. To toy with him. To tempt him. Ezra was more than willing to play along. In the end, they would all have what they wanted. What they needed.

"I like it when you both touch me," Anna continued, and leaned up to pepper light kisses against his neck.

Ezra didn't look at her, but at Oliver, holding his gaze steadily. "And have you ever been shared?"

He felt Anna stiffen at his side. "No," she whispered. Whimpered.

"Would you like it?" Ezra asked. Asked her. Asked Oliver, too.

Oliver was nodding as Anna said, "Yes."

"We could do that here," Ezra said. "But because this isn't for the painting...it is most definitely purely for my pleasure, and both of yours, I'd like to go back to my bedroom. And I want to share her with you, Oliver."

"I want that too," Oliver croaked.

Ezra smiled and then, without warning, he swept Anna up, tossing her over his shoulder like he was a conquering Viking about to claim his plunder. She squealed in arousal and delight, laughing as he carried her across the room. Her laughter faded when he caressed her backside through the silky robe. Then she moaned.

And he knew he was about to have an explosive morning.

CHAPTER 8

Oliver

Oliver was shaking as he followed Ezra into the other man's room and watched as he tossed Anna back onto the bed where they had all slept the night before. Oliver had the powerful knowledge that he didn't belong here, that he wasn't worthy of the pleasures both these remarkable people wanted to share with him.

But he didn't leave. He couldn't. Not when he was getting to live out his every wicked fantasy. He pushed the thoughts from his head and moved toward Anna, untying her robe gently and lowering it from her shoulders so that she was naked again. He would never grow accustomed to getting to see her like this. It would always be a stunning dream that he feared he would wake from.

Ezra removed his trousers quickly and that was a dream too. Oliver had been with his first man a decade before, but those encounters were nothing like what he'd felt with Ezra. This was no quick exchange of pleasure in the dark. This was something else.

But he couldn't dwell on that or analyze it. So he pushed it away and leaned down to kiss Anna. She lifted against him, murmuring softly and tickling his lips with her soft breath. The kiss slowed and deepened, and he drowned in the feel of her, the taste of her.

"Give her to me," Ezra said, moving to stand behind Anna, letting his hands trail over her skin. His fingers brushed Oliver's as they crossed, and Oliver shivered as he pulled away. There was a possessive glitter in the other man's stare, something dark and needy and it stirred jealousy and desire in equal measure.

Slowly, he turned Anna toward Ezra and she wrapped her arms around his bare shoulders and lifted into his mouth without hesitation. Before Ezra kissed her, he arched a brow at Oliver. "Undress."

That commanding tone dragged along Oliver's spine and he followed it instantly, stripping out of his clothing without taking his eyes off of the couple before him. Anna and Ezra kissed passionately, their tongues warring. She began to lift against him, making those little gasps and moans that were like music to Oliver's ears.

When Oliver was naked, Ezra crooked his finger and motioned him toward their tangled bodies. Oliver came and settled himself behind Anna now, resting one hand on Ezra's shoulder and the other on her bare hip. They both shuddered at his touch, and Anna broke from the kiss to turn her face upward and look at Oliver.

"Please," she whimpered, grinding so her bare backside stroked against his already hard cock. The sensation rushed up the staff, settled in his balls, spread throughout every nerve ending of his very aware body.

And oh, how he wanted to fuck her. Hard and fast while Ezra watched, harder and faster while he joined. He wanted to feel Ezra's cock in her, stroking against his own. He wanted it all and it felt decadent and greedy to allow himself that desire.

"Has anyone ever fucked your arse, Anna?" Ezra asked, leaning close to her ear, nibbling there gently even as he let his hand trail along Oliver's side.

Anna pushed back against Oliver again with a little moan. "Yes," she admitted. "A few times."

"Did you like it?"

She swallowed and then she nodded, even as her cheeks flamed. "When I was readied enough, yes. I liked it very much."

"Well, we are going to ready you," Ezra said with a chuckle. "Until you beg. Isn't that right, Oliver?"

Oliver could hardly breathe, let alone speak, but somehow he managed to nod.

Ezra arched a brow. "Say it," he said.

Oliver's voice shook, but he choked out, "Yes."

Anna reached back, clenching at Oliver's naked hip even as she lifted up to kiss Ezra again. He broke the kiss after a moment and smiled at her. "Lean over the bed, please."

Oliver let her go and she did as she'd been asked, bending over the edge of the bed and giving him the most gorgeous view of her from behind. He rested a hand on the globe of her arse, stroking the soft skin there as she ground against the bed.

Meanwhile, he watched Ezra move to his bedside table and open a drawer. He withdrew a small bottle of oil of some kind and brought it back to Oliver. He handed it over with a grin. "I think you deserve the honor."

Oliver drew a shaky breath as he poured a little oil on his fingertips. He rolled it between them to warm it and then gently probed the tips between her cheeks, finding the tight entrance and slowly massaging it.

She gripped the edge of the bed with a little cry of pleasure and looked back over her shoulder with eyes bright with desire. Ezra eased between the edge of the bed and her body and caught her chin, lifting it so she looked at him.

"Make me hard, Anna," he ordered.

She smiled as he bounced free. "You're already hard," she whispered, but it didn't stop her from catching his length in her hand and stroking over him.

Oliver exhaled shakily, pumping his fingers into her tight entrance as he watched her take Ezra into her mouth. She sucked and licked him as Ezra leaned back on his hands, flexing his hips to make her take him farther, fucking her mouth like they would soon both fuck her body.

As Oliver continued to ready her arse, he reached around with his other hand and stroked her pussy. He found her wet, hot, needy and ready. She shivered as he now filled both her holes, pumping in with one finger and out with the other. He could feel the digits rub against each other as he did so and imagined his cock and Ezra's doing the same. He could almost come just picturing it.

Oliver lost track of time as they all pleasured each other in the quiet room. Nothing mattered but this. Nothing would ever matter again. But at last Ezra dragged his fingers through Anna's tangled hair, tilting her mouth off of him and forcing her to look at him again.

"Now," he said, with no further explanation. Not that he needed it. Anna seemed eager, hungry, as she pushed Ezra back on the bed and pressed her knee on the mattress next to his hip. Oliver's fingers slipped from her backside and she grunted, even as she straddled Ezra and slowly eased his cock into her body.

She ground down with a whine of pleasure, then eased to stillness as she looked over her shoulder at Oliver.

He moved forward. Ezra opened his legs a little to give him a space and he took it, rubbing the head of his cock against her tight hole. She pressed back and he began to ease inside the impossibly taut channel. She felt full from the press of Ezra's cock inside her pussy and Oliver took his time, easing past resistance as she wailed.

He felt them both against him and the pleasure was almost too much. He gripped her hips, digging his fingers into her flesh as she rocked against him, then he lost himself to pleasure. Hers. Ezra's. His own.

For that moment, it was all that mattered.

~

Anna

Anna had experienced pleasure in her life, but the intensity of the sensation of being filled by these two men was so powerful that it bordered on unbearable. Every nerve in her entire body felt like it was firing at once and she was so aware of her body being stretched that she almost couldn't breathe.

"Look at me," Ezra moaned. She opened her eyes, which she hadn't even fully realized were squeezed shut, and looked down at him. His blue gaze held hers, calming, soothing, arousing and she found some center again. He nodded as if he saw that. "Ride me. Slowly."

She began to rise and fall against him, rocking her clitoris against his pelvis and multiplying the pleasure. Behind her, Oliver also began to move, thrusting into her backside in time to her movements as his fingers dug into her hips.

Everything in the world spiraled down, the focus becoming pinpointed on their bodies and what it felt like to be taken by both of them. She pressed her palms into Ezra's chest, balancing against his firm presence, locking her eyes with his bright ones as they all moved together as one sleek, powerful animal that only existed for sensation.

The edge of her orgasm was right there as the two men worked in tandem for her pleasure. Ezra cupped her breasts from below, stroking his thumbs around her sensitive nipples. Meanwhile Oliver metered his strokes so that he pulled back from her every time that Ezra lifted. The result was that she was always being filled, stroked.

She threw her head back, resting it against Oliver's straining shoulder. She didn't try to contain her gasps and cries of pleasure as she began to quake with pleasure. It hit her in waves, harder than anything she'd ever felt before, and she shattered, screaming out incoherently.

And as she did so, she felt Ezra's strokes change, felt him come to the edge himself. Felt Oliver do the same. She gripped her hands against Ezra's chest tighter.

"Come in me, please!" she gasped out. Ezra's eyes went wide, but she shook her head. "I can't have children. Please, I want to feel it."

He lifted harder and then came, flooding her clenching sheath. And as if the ripples drew Oliver's pleasure, he swiftly followed. They stayed as they were for a moment, Anna collapsed over Ezra's chest, Oliver curled around her back. Their panting breaths became matched, slowed, and only then did Oliver rise and gently ease from her. Her legs shook as he helped her off of Ezra to lie on the bed.

While Ezra shifted her to the pillows and then curled her into his side, Oliver moved to the basin of clean water on a table across the room. He wiped himself off, then brought a fresh cloth over. Gently, he tended to her until she was clean. He pressed a kiss to her shoulder and then returned to the basin to rinse the cloths and set them to dry before the fire.

"How do you know you cannot have children?" Ezra asked gently.

Anna froze, her attention to Oliver drawn away even though she saw him stiffen. She cleared her throat. "My husband had several illegitimate children with multiple mistresses. It is evident his seed was not the reason he and I could not have children of our own."

Ezra glanced down at her, his concern for her plain on his handsome face. "It hurt you."

"That he flaunted his bastards, certainly...at first," she said with a sigh and a blush.

Oliver returned to them then and joined them on the bed, wrapping his body behind hers. She felt so safe cradled between them, their arms tangled through each other's and around her. Like nothing bad could ever happen. It made her want to be honest because vulnerability didn't seem like a trap in this quiet room with these amazing men.

"As far as sadness over my inability to breed...no," she admitted. "Some may think that strange, but I have never felt a calling to be a mother. I don't dislike children. A chubby baby is adorable, and bright, quizzical children are always entertaining. But I've never longed to have my own." She glanced up at Ezra, searching his face to see if he thought her less because of that. Certainly her husband had.

But he didn't look shocked or horrified at all. He was nodding, in fact, as if he understood that lack of desire to do what so many insisted was the only natural thing. "Society does press, but there is something thrilling about independence."

Behind her, Oliver grunted, and Anna felt the tension in him increase. "As if that horse's arse would ever grant her independence," he muttered, and for the first time ever Anna heard his anger at the late duke. His disdain for his former master.

She shifted slightly toward him and looked at Oliver's face, now lined with protectiveness...and regret. He shook his head. "I'm sorry, I said too much."

"It must have been difficult for you to see how she was hurt," Ezra said carefully.

Oliver nodded slowly. "I hated every moment of it."

Anna cupped his cheek and leaned up to kiss him. A swell of emotion filled her chest. She knew what it was, that dangerous desire that went beyond the physical. That secret voice that whispered about a future she feared couldn't be possible.

So she pushed it away. "The benefit, of course," she teased, dragging her fingers up Oliver's arm as she gently pulsed back against Ezra's body, "is that you two may spend it me as you please. Just as you did today."

Oliver's pupils dilated and a possessive hunger filled them at that suggestion. Like he could claim her. Oh, how she wanted him to claim her. To use her. To let down the servant's mask and let her give to him as he had relentlessly given to her over the years.

"You can grind against me all you like, my delightful little minx," Ezra said, leaning forward to nip her earlobe. "But a man does need time to recover before we play again. I suggest we all have a nice rest, a good breakfast…and then…"

"Then?" Anna whispered, glancing over her shoulder at him.

Ezra leaned over, past her, and kissed first Oliver, then turned his head to do the same to her. "And then I'm going to expect an intense afternoon together."

Anna smiled at the suggestion, the thrill in her chest undeniable. She snuggled against Oliver, wedged against Ezra and to her surprise, she very swiftly slipped back into a dreamless sleep. And it was just like heaven.

CHAPTER 9

Oliver

The next few days felt like a blur. A delicious, erotic blur that Oliver would cherish for the rest of his days. He kept waiting for this to be over. For Anna to suggest they continue on their way or go back to London. Or for Ezra to imply that he was finished with the game.

Only none of that happened. The roads were clear now, the air crisp but bright with sunshine. Yet each afternoon Ezra suggested they stay. And Anna agreed.

Ezra would paint them, breathing heavily as Oliver brought Anna to orgasm over and over, reveling in her taste and her scent and the way she shook around his body when she came in long, powerful waves. Then Ezra would join them and they would sink into each other, a puddle of arms and legs and cocks. Oliver was learning how both his lovers liked to be touched. He was reveling in how easy it was to make their respective breaths catch and legs shake.

It was magical. But Oliver knew it would end. He could pretend all he liked that he belonged with these two people, but he didn't. He was a servant. He'd been raised by a servant to become a servant and live his entire life that way. At some point they would remember. At some point he would be dismissed and everyone's life would move on.

That thought caused him pain and his long strides down the hallway faltered a little before he measured his response. He had been looking for Anna and Ezra for a few moments and couldn't show his emotions when he found them.

He entered the studio and smiled, the fears and concerns dissipating naturally as he saw Anna standing at the window, bright sunshine falling over her face. For a moment she didn't notice his entrance and he could just drink her in.

She was so entirely beautiful, both inside and out. He adored her beyond reason, loved her to distraction. A love that only grew the more they were able to share themselves with each other. Sometimes, when the moonlight would stream through the windows into Ezra's room and hit her sleeping form, Oliver actually...ached.

"Good afternoon," Anna said, turning toward him with a bright smile that was so warm. "You look very handsome, as usual."

He smiled and crossed the room to her, heart skipping as she opened her arms and wrapped them around him. They kissed, her body sagging against his and she sighed with contentment. She didn't exit his embrace as she looked up at his face.

"Have you seen Ezra?" she asked.

He shook his head. "No, I thought you'd be together."

It was funny, his reaction to that concept. Part of him loved watching Anna with Ezra. Their connection was growing more powerful each day and certainly the other man knew how to please her. Anna being pleased was infinitely arousing.

But there was another part that was jealous. Just a kernel of that negative feeling.

"I assumed he'd be here, working on the piece," she said, and motioned toward two canvases close by. They were both covered with cloths so one couldn't see the image beneath. Anna slid her fingers along Oliver's arm. "Should we peek?" she asked.

His eyes widened at the thought. "Ezra hasn't shown us yet—do you think he'd want that?"

Anna's bottom lip stuck out in a playful pout. "I only want to look," she said. "After all, the piece is you and me, we deserve to know, don't we?"

He choked back a laugh as she leaned against him. She did know how to get a man on her side of an issues. "I suppose," he conceded softly, "that as the subjects of the piece, we could argue we ought to be able to see it."

She smiled broadly. "Good!" She moved to the two canvases and stared. "I wonder which one it is? Do you think he's working on two pieces?"

"I have no idea," Oliver asked as he watched her, amused by her enthusiasm. "I suppose there is only one way to find out. Pick one."

She looked at him over her shoulder with a wicked expression. "Oh, if there's one thing you two have taught me, it's that I never have to pick just one."

With that she tugged the cloths from both canvases and together they stared. The painting on the right was the one they'd posing for, and both of them caught their breath at once.

The image was beautiful. In it, Anna was straddled over Oliver, his mouth against her breast, her fingers dug into his hair. He couldn't almost feel the pressure of them, it was so real. Her head was thrown back and to the side so that her face couldn't be seen or identified, but the passion was evident either way.

Her hand trembled as she extended it and then let it drop without touching the image. "Oh," she breathed, her voice shaking. "It's...it's wonderful."

"Yes," he agreed, and swallowed hard. Was this how they looked when they were tangled? It was glorious and arousing.

And he would have been aroused except for one problem: Ezra hadn't just captured the intimacy of their physical joining, he'd captured something else, too.

While Anna's face was turned so that her identity would be protected, Oliver's was clear The image of him captured his face upturned, mouth latched against her breast, yes, but his gaze was focused on her. And the fact that he loved her was plain as the color of his hair or the arch of her back.

He swallowed hard at seeing the naked emotion there. The naked love and pain and hope and fear all streaked across the lines of his face.

"Who…who is she?" Anna said softly.

Oliver forced himself to stop looking at the portrait of them and to the other picture that had been covered. It wasn't, as he had expected, of him and Anna. No, this was a different woman with black hair and green eyes. She was posed on her knees, lifted up slightly, looking straight on toward the artist. She was naked, but she held a blanket up to partly cover herself. It fell between her legs, giving some tiny scrap of modesty.

Anna moved closer. "She's beautiful," she breathed. "Almost alive."

"She is," Oliver agreed. "I wonder what—"

He didn't get to finish because at that moment, the door behind them slammed. They both turned to find Ezra standing there, his face pale, his eyes wide and his hands shaking at his sides.

"What the hell are you doing?"

Ezra

Ezra could barely stay upright as he strode across the room and jerked the cloth back up to cover the portrait Oliver and Anna had been looking at. He pivoted back and glared at them.

"These are my private things," he snapped, wishing his voice didn't shake.

"Ezra," Anna said softly. "We...*I*...only wanted to see the portrait you created of us. I was curious."

"You had no right," Ezra said.

Oliver moved forward, positioning himself slightly in front of Anna. "Watch your tone," he said, gently but firmly.

Ezra blinked and realized how sharp he'd sounded. How loud. He hadn't meant to shout. To overreact. "I-I'm sorry," he whispered.

Anna shook her head. "You needn't be." She squeezed Oliver's arm as she slipped around him. She touched Ezra's cheek gently and he let his breath come out in a shuddering sigh. How strange that he could be so soothed by a person he hadn't even known a week before. "The portrait of Oliver and me is beautiful."

He nodded. "I-I was going to show it to you soon."

"But that isn't why you're upset," Anna continued, her voice gentle.

He caught his breath again and stared past her at the shrouded canvas. He could cover it all he liked. He couldn't unsee it. Unfeel what it made him feel to paint it. To look at it. That was always with him.

"Who was she?" Anna asked.

Ezra hesitated. Did he want to tell Oliver and Anna the truth? Did he want to strip himself down emotionally as much as he had already done physically with these two people? When he truly considered that, the answer was...

Yes.

He extended a hand and gently tugged the cloths back down

from both the pieces. Next to each other, they both told a story. Very different stories, but each featuring people who played important roles along the timeline of his life. Anna squeezed his hand and then moved back toward the portrait, staring closer at the image Ezra had so carefully and lovingly created.

He could hardly breathe as he watched her, as he felt Oliver's eyes on him. He didn't show this pain, not to anyone. And yet it felt so close to the surface in that moment. So near to these two people who had so unexpectedly come into his life and reawakened his creativity and his true, deep passion.

"Her name was Beatrice," he said, his voice rougher than he wanted it to be. "She was…I loved her. I would have married her, against my father's wishes, against my grandfather's threats." He shook his head as his mind took him back, back to those heady days. Those horrible days.

"Who was she that they would not allow you to be happy?" Oliver pressed gently.

Ezra looked at him, realizing that the answer would be very stark to this man who believed he could not have happiness because of his position in the world. "An actress. She used to pose for me in the early days when I was developing as an artist."

His mind swirled him off to heady days and nights with Beatrice. With her laugh and her smile and her encouragement that had helped him become the man he was today.

"What happened to her?" Anna whispered, lifting her gaze to him.

"She died," he choked out. "She got very sick, and she died. Five years ago."

From behind him, Oliver made a soft, choked sound of pain and Ezra felt him move even before Oliver touched him. The other man's fingers tightened around his forearm and it was…comforting.

"I'm sorry," Oliver said.

Ezra nodded. "Yes. Everyone is sorry. I'm sorry. Her life was far too brief and far too difficult. Her death...changed me."

"How so?" Anna asked, stepping closer and taking his other hand. He was suddenly surrounded by them, enclosed in a protective circle of their warmth and empathy. Safe. When was the last time he'd felt safe?

"I used to paint for myself," he said, feeling the hollowness. "And I couldn't anymore after she died. Every piece I've done has been a commission since then. Until..."

He trailed off and they both turned to look at the nearly finished portrait of Anna and Oliver. Of their passion. Ezra's image wasn't in the painting, but he felt himself there, just beyond the edges of the frame, watching them in their pleasure, in their passion, in their love.

Anna's expression softened and she edged a little closer. "I'm sure she would love that you were creating for yourself again, Ezra. If she cared for you the way you cared for her, she would want you to be happy."

"She would," he agreed. "I've struggled with that a long time. Struggled with all I could have done to make things better for her. To be braver for her. But right here, with you two...all I can recall is how lovely she was. And bright and talented. There was no one better who ever walked the boards." He blinked at the tears that suddenly filled his eyes. "And also how she smiled when I was happy."

Oliver cleared his throat. "Then she most definitely loved you."

Ezra looked at him. If anyone would know, it was Oliver, who would throw himself down a mine shaft for Anna, asking nothing in return.

"I'm...glad you looked at it," he said softly, speaking to them both even as he kept looking at Oliver. "After all we've shared, I think you should understand this."

"Is this why you left London?" Anna asked. "Separated yourself from your family."

"My father and grandfather all but crowed when she died," Ezra said, his voice hollow. "They celebrated and insisted I go straight back to the marriage mart and follow their desired arrangements. Give up painting."

"Bastards," Oliver muttered, and for a moment he wasn't a servant, he was only Ezra's protective lover. And Ezra almost couldn't breathe because that was so powerful.

He stepped away from Beatrice's portrait and reached out to touch Oliver's face. The roughness of his beard tickled Ezra's palm.

"Always the protector," he said softly. "And it is so lovely, to feel that. I'm almost jealous that Anna has been able to experience it for so very long."

Oliver shifted and Ezra could see the vulnerability that statement created. Oliver wanted to fade into the background, as he likely believed a man of his position should. To do for others and never be noticed for it.

But Ezra noticed. Appreciated. Adored, it turned out. When he looked into this man's warm, brown eyes, he truly adored him. More to the point, he wanted Oliver. To have him. To claim him. To bind himself to him and feel the comfort that his steady presence provided. In this moment, when he still stung from memories, he needed that.

"When I'm with you, it helps me...not forget." He shook his head. "But you've made it easier. The pleasure, the desire...the connection, it makes it easier."

Oliver's expression softened. "I'm glad. You deserve for everything to be easier. To have pleasure sweep you away."

Ezra swallowed hard. "Have you had a man take you?"

He heard Anna suck in her breath, but didn't look at her. He knew she celebrated the bond between Ezra and Oliver as deeply as she celebrated their passion for her. If she reacted, it was because she knew that this question opened a door to a new level of connection between them all.

Oliver jerked out a shaky nod. "Yes," he whispered.

"Could I…" Ezra began. Before he could finish, Oliver nodded again, this time with confidence.

"Yes!" he gasped.

Ezra found himself smiling, a shock considering he'd just been discussing Beatrice and that topic tended to throw him into despair. But right now he felt connected to Oliver, to Anna, to the passion that pulsed between them. And touching this man would ease the pain, would make everything better.

Forever.

He blinked as he pushed that thought away. He ignored it as he reached out to take Oliver's hand. "Come with me. Both of you."

Anna

Watching Ezra guide Oliver into his bedroom, standing aside as he pushed him against the door to shut it and then kissed Oliver just as passionately as he had ever kissed her... it was exciting. She loved watching these two men as they moved together, their bodies grinding, their hands roving. Their passion for each other took nothing away from their passion for her or hers for them. It only added to the bond they shared, both individually and as a group.

Oliver made a sound low in his throat as Ezra's mouth moved to his neck, his shoulder. He was already tugging at Oliver's clothing, stripping him down in a few expert movements. He flattened his hand against Oliver's bare ribcage, fingers raking across the lines of bone and muscle, and the sound Oliver made was barely human. His hips jolted against Ezra's and Ezra let out a low chuckle.

He wrapped his hand around Oliver's cock and began to stroke. Oliver's head lolled back, rapping against the door behind him. Anna was captivated. He didn't allow for this, not usually. If he had pleasure, it was always the byproduct of giving it. He didn't allow her or Ezra to touch him just for his own pleasure. But right now he lifted his hips, panting as Ezra expertly tugged at him.

She couldn't breathe as she waited for what would happen next. Waited for Oliver's control to break. But he didn't allow it. Suddenly his dark eyes flew open and he jolted against Ezra's chest. His hand slid down and he unfastened Ezra's trousers, freeing his cock.

"What are you doing?" Ezra murmured, his fingers faltering in their work.

"Readying you," Oliver whispered back. "So you can have me."

Ezra laughed and nuzzled Oliver's neck gently. "I think you can feel I'm very ready as it is."

Anna looked at it was, indeed, true. Ezra was hard as steel already. But Oliver kept stroking, focusing his attention on that action, rather than on the hand that still fought to pleasure him.

Ezra let out a little sigh and glanced at Anna. "Do you remember the oil?"

She tried to focus on the question and jerked out a nod. "In... in the bedside table?"

He smiled. "Yes. Bring it to me. And undress."

He was undeniable, as always. She did as she was told without question, bringing him the bottle of oil and stripping before she stepped back to her place before them so she could watch. So she could see every moment of what would happen next as Ezra got ready to fuck Oliver's arse the same way both men had taken turns claiming hers over the past few days.

"Stand in front of him," Ezra ordered, and Oliver eased away from the edge of the bed to give her a space. She lifted up and wrapped her arms around him, kissing him as he bent her over the bed to offer his backside to Ezra.

She sank into the kiss, reveling in it as she always did. It never seemed entirely real, more like something out of a fairytale. A very wicked fairytale, considering that when she pulled away and opened her eyes, it was to see Ezra gently working his fingers between the cheeks of Oliver's backside.

Oliver moaned and rested his forehead against her shoulder. She held him, smoothing her fingers through his hair. "Isn't he magical?" she murmured into his ear, nipping the lobe. "So good at that."

Oliver nodded without lifting his head. "So good," he repeated, his voice broken.

"Just wait until he takes you," she whispered, and loved how Oliver's hands gripped the coverlet, clenching for purchase. "I can't wait to see it."

Ezra was pumping his fingers into Oliver now, pressing him wider with one hand even as he stroked his own cock, coating it with oil with the other. "Watch," he murmured, locking eyes with her.

She nodded and stared as Ezra aligned himself with Oliver. Oliver whimpered as Ezra took him. An inch. Two. Then all of him in a slick slide. When Ezra was fully seated, his hips touching Oliver's, Oliver shuddered and lifted his head. His mouth was slightly open, his pupils dilated with pleasure, his entire body quivering with it.

Ezra began to grind his hips, slow at first, letting Oliver feel the stretch of him. Anna knew exactly what that felt like, having that big cock inside of her just like that. Feeling the press of his fingers against her hips.

"Does it feel good?" she panted, putting two fingers under Oliver's chin and lifting so that he looked at her.

"Yes," he groaned, his tone garbled.

She smiled and then shifted so she could slide her hand down his chest. She caught his cock and stroked. Oliver grunted, swore under his breath, pushed his hand hard against her palm. Then he shook his head and tried to shove her hand away.

She wrinkled her brow. He wanted this. She could see it. He

wanted her to make him come while Ezra fucked him, harder now, gasping and moaning at the pleasure of it.

But he wouldn't let her. And not for the first time, it frustrated her. He would give, oh yes. He would give until she was so satisfied that she couldn't move. But he never allowed her the pleasure in return. He never gave himself completely.

And she feared, in that heated moment. That he never would.

~

Ezra

Although it was hard to focus with Oliver's tight backside gripping his cock with every stroke, Ezra could see that Anna was frustrated. Aroused, hungry, gorgeous…but frustrated as Oliver refused her.

"I want to make you come," Anna panted, desperate, needy as she tried to stoke him again. Oliver caught her hand and shook his head.

"No," he grunted, pushing her back on the bed.

She fell back without a fight. He mumbled something incoherent and pushed her legs open, his body trembling as he stared down at her. Ezra did the same over his shoulders, staring at the slick evidence of Anna's desire for Oliver, even with another man's cock buried deep inside of him. He slowed his thrusts behind Oliver, savoring the clench of the other man around him, the building pleasure that zipped through him like a lightning bolt and moved toward a powerful crescendo.

Oliver made a low growl, as close to possessive as the man ever let himself be. He pressed hand on either side of Anna's hips at the edge of the bed, leaned farther forward and buried his head between her legs.

Anna whimpered, but her frustration remained as plain as her desire. Ezra understood it—hell, he felt it too. Oliver was amazing at giving pleasure, at serving his lovers. But he wouldn't let them return that pleasure. Some part of him held himself separate. He'd done so when Ezra had him pressed against the door and was stroking him. He'd done so when Anna practically begged him to let her suck him.

As if Oliver could read their mutual thoughts, he began to circle Anna's clitoris with his tongue and she writhed on the bed. At the same time, he pulsed back against Ezra, gripping him all the tighter with his arse.

Thoughts faded as sensation took over. Ezra's fingers dug harder into Oliver's hips, denting the firm flesh there. Possibly marking him with finger bruises. Claiming him at last.

"Fuck, oh fuck," he grunted, sweat beading against his brow when the pleasure spiraled higher and higher, out of control. He felt his cock begin to pulse and then he came. He howled Oliver's name, his head thrown back, his eyes squeezed shut.

Anna whimpered and Ezra opened his eyes to watch her come, too. Her hips jolted as pleasure rocked through her. Oliver drew it out, moaning against her as she came, body twitching and twisting beneath him. Then he collapsed against her on the bed, holding her without asking for his hard cock to be relieved.

Ezra slowly withdrew, watching beads of his come slide down the back of Oliver's thighs. God, how he wanted to paint that image. The aftermath of pleasure.

Anna scooted over a little and Oliver curled beside her, still half on and half off the high bed. He flopped an arm over her stomach, watching her, but Anna turned her face. Ezra frowned. This was more than frustration. Oliver's resistance really hurt her.

And he supposed, if he allowed this connection between them to continue, to grow…it would eventually hurt him, too. So perhaps it was time to address it. Once and for all.

He walked to the door, feeling both of them track him like

hungry wolves. With a smile, he reached up and pulled the bell. As he waited, he glanced back at his two lovers, naked on his bed.

"Why don't we have a bath?" he suggested. "And then a very long talk."

CHAPTER 11

Anna

Anna had expected there would be distractions in bathing with these two men. And there had been, at least a little. Ezra had soaked in the tub with her first, washing himself and rubbing her body, smiling when she gasped and moaned for him. But he hadn't pushed past just teasing.

Then Oliver joined her, washing swiftly before he positioned himself behind her. And now Anna shivered as Oliver worked the soap through her hair gently, his fingers caressing her scalp.

"Oh, it has been far too long since someone did that," she murmured.

Ezra shifted in his spot in a chair beside the tub, and she felt him looking at her even though she didn't open her eyes. She wished she could take the words back, erase his interest. She didn't want to tell this man the entire story. To make him pity her, as she was sure he would pity her.

"Why is that?" he asked gently. "As a duchess, you must have servants lined up to take care of you." She didn't answer and he cleared his throat. "Anna," he said.

She opened her eyes at last and found herself speared by his gaze. She felt Oliver's fingers tighten a little against her skin, his tension matching hers, just as it always seemed to.

"Why didn't you have any other servants when you came here?" Ezra pressed.

"Because…because when my husband died, he made no arrangements for my being taken care of," she admitted, hating how her voice cracked. "And the new duke stopped paying my servants months ago, so they left."

Ezra's expression darkened with anger. Frustration on her behalf. He glanced past her to Oliver. "And why did he continue to pay you?"

Anna looked up at Oliver to see his answer, and in that moment she saw a flutter cross his expression. She sat up and twisted to face him. "O-Oliver?"

"He *didn't* pay you, did he?" Ezra whispered.

Oliver didn't say anything, but used the pitcher to rinse her hair. She caught his hand after he was finished and held it tightly. "Oliver. Did he pay you?"

"No," Oliver said, and met her eyes evenly.

She shook her head as the truth of that statement rushed through her. The rest of her servants had departed at least two months ago due to lack of funds. The idea that Oliver had been unpaid since that same time…

"No. No. Oliver, why did you stay?" she asked.

He cupped her cheek, smoothing rivulets of water from her skin with his thumb. "You know why," he said, his low voice breaking.

Tears leapt to her eyes. Yes. She did know why. Of course she did. She knew this man, this marvelous, wonderful man cared deeply for her. Perhaps even loved her, not that she deserved the heart that beat in his chest. He was ten times the man as any she'd ever met. Worthy of more than she could give in a hundred lifetimes, a thousand.

"Oliver," she began.

He shook his head and got up, pushing out of the tub in one smooth motion and leaving her behind to stare as he caught a towel and began drying himself swiftly. He refused to look at her now, refused to look at Ezra.

"I shouldn't have said anything," he said.

She shook her head and stood, as well. Ezra helped her from the tub and handed over a towel for her, too. She wrapped it around herself. "It turns out you *didn't* say anything," she argued. "You kept the truth from me for months while you took over every single duty of every servant who had departed. From cook to household manager."

"And I should have continued to do so," Oliver insisted. "What bloody good does it do anyway?"

She moved forward and caught his damp arm, forcing him to look at her. When he did, his expression was deeply pained. She hesitated at it. This was what she did to him. She hurt him. Without meaning to, of course. She would never hurt him on purpose.

"Oliver," she whispered, touching his rough cheek.

"No," he muttered, and pulled away gently. "Just let it be, Anna. We got this time together, didn't we? We got this moment. It was more than I ever could have asked for. Let's not push it."

He walked away then, back into the bedroom. As he did so, Anna looked at Ezra. He seemed as troubled by this as she was, even though he had known them for far less time. But he was bound to them now. There was no denying that anymore.

"What do I do?" she whispered.

He shook his head. "Don't let him go," he suggested. "Don't let him put up this wall or I fear neither of us will ever scale it."

She nodded, shoving her shoulders back like she was preparing for war, and perhaps she was. She marched into the room, hoping she looked more certain than she felt. Right now she just felt afraid. Afraid that she would do something that would spoil this and lose Oliver forever.

"I want to push it," she said, repeating the phrasing Oliver had used a moment before. "Because you are worth it. What we share is worth it. Or don't you agree?"

Oliver was standing next to the bed and he froze, dropping his head. "Anna," he said softly.

She ignored the plea in his tone. "You want me, I know you do. You've proven that regularly during these last few wonderful days. But it's more than that. What you did for me before my husband's death…"

"Devouring your pussy in a hallway like a starving animal?" Oliver snapped.

She nodded. "Yes. But that's not what I meant. I meant the way you watched over me. The way you showed me you were there in actions. The way you made me feel safe when nothing was safe."

"Anna," Oliver said again, and his voice was more strained.

Once again, she ignored him. "Do you think I want to lose that? Do you think I want to forget it and go back to anything like what used to be? Why would I want to do that? Why would you?"

"Stop!" Oliver said at last, pivoting to face her. He stepped forward and caught her arms gently, dragging her closer. "Why are you pretending you don't understand why, Anna? Why are you pretending I'm not a servant?"

Oliver

For a moment the words hung in the air between them. Anna stared up at him, her breath short.

"But you're not a servant anymore," Anna said at last, then her dark blue eyes scanned over his body with a hungry look that spoke to his own deep desire. Sparked the love he felt for her that could never be. "If the new duke isn't paying you, then you aren't a servant."

"I'll always be a servant," he choked out as he released her, finger by finger.

Ezra's low laugh from the corner shocked its way through Oliver's blood and he slowly trailed his gaze to the other man. God's teeth but he was a sight to behold, leaning against the wall, his muscled arms folded across his bare chest and his hair tousled from everything they'd been doing that long, passionate day.

And Oliver wanted him, just like he wanted Anna as she raked her nails across his chest and practically arched against him like a cat.

"That doesn't have to be true," Ezra said, pushing off the wall and stalking toward him. "And in some ways I think it's how you hide. From her. From me. From yourself."

"Easily said by a man who's always had everything he ever wanted," Oliver retorted.

Anna's fingers hesitated and Ezra stopped moving toward him. He cocked his head. "I have been lucky, privileged," he conceded softly. "But you are being offered everything you ever wanted right now." He nodded his head toward Anna. "If you let go and let her. Let me. We would give you *everything*."

Anna pushed Oliver back and he hit the edge of the bed. He had two choices then: to deny them both or to lie down. With a shuddering sigh, he chose the second. Because no matter how he tried to fight this, he was too weak.

Slowly, Anna climbed up on the bed and knelt between his legs, her hands against his thighs. "Let us," she repeated, her voice hypnotic and erotic and filled with such sensual promise that he went hard as stone almost instantly.

"Please," Ezra said. His voice was rough and it felt like it dragged along Oliver's spine in the most delicious way.

Oliver didn't answer. Words seemed too vulnerable at the moment. But he did let out his breath in a shaking sigh and shut his eyes. Silent acquiescence. At least for a moment. He would take what they offered for a moment, before it was torn away.

"Oliver," Anna whispered. "Look at me. Watch me."

He opened his eyes slowly and stared as she lowered her head to stroke her cheek against his bare thigh. Ezra made a soft sound and came to stand beside the bed. He gathered the length of her hair and wrapped it around his fist so that Oliver's view of her was no longer obstructed. Anna made a little sound at the back of her throat and slid her hands up the front of Oliver's thighs.

"I want you to see what I'm going to do to you," she murmured as she gripped the base of his cock.

He jolted at her touch. He always did. He always would. He had a feeling he would jolt at the memory of it, even after she was long gone from his life. But he didn't want to think about that now. He only wanted to think about her lips moving toward his length. He only wanted to think about how good it felt when she darted out her pink tongue and glided it around the tip.

"Fuck," he grunted, lifting his hips.

Ezra chuckled and with the hand that wasn't holding her hair, he pressed a palm to Oliver's stomach, then lower where he held him steady. "No one tells the lady how fast to move. Give in, Oliver."

Oliver met the other man's eyes and then pressed his hips up again, into Ezra's weight. He rotated them slowly, daring Ezra to do something about it. Oh so very ready for whatever that punishment would be.

Ezra's pupils dilated with his defiance and his lips quirked up in a smile. "Anna, my dear?"

Anna glanced up from her work at Oliver's cock. "Yes?"

"I want you to make this very naughty man writhe." He returned his gaze to Oliver. "I want you to make him quake."

"With great pleasure," Anna murmured, and took Oliver into her mouth fully. He cried out as she drew him into her throat instantly, swirling her tongue around him as she sucked.

He almost couldn't see, couldn't think and it took all of whatever focus he had left to note that Ezra was pushing her hair aside, over her shoulder so Oliver continued to have a clear view of her mouth on his cock. But Ezra let her go and he climbed up on the bed, resting on his side next to Oliver. His hand slid up Oliver's body, tracing little patterns over his skin.

"Give in," he whispered, pressing his lips to Oliver's shoulder. His tongue was hot against the flesh and Oliver's vision blurred at the feeling of both their mouths on him. Sucking, licking, pleasuring like he was the center of the world. Like he was everything.

He'd never been everything before. It was overwhelming and wonderful and he never wanted them to stop.

Luckily they didn't. Anna began to stroke over him, all the way to the root until she almost choked, then back to gasp out a breath. Her tongue lapped ceaselessly, her hand pulsed around him. She took him to the edge of madness and then slowly drew him back, not letting him find that ultimate pleasure until she was ready.

And while she did that, while she tormented him, Ezra nuzzled his neck, sucking the skin there, nibbling along the column of his neck until he found Oliver's mouth. His rough tongue stroked over Oliver's in deep, hard thrusts and the room disappeared so there was only sensation.

Sensation that washed away reason, that built with powerful speed in his loins and sent tingles to every nerve ending in his sensitive body. He found himself moaning into Ezra's mouth, his fingers gripping at the sheets, his hips tensing in time to the long, steady pulls of Anna's gorgeous mouth.

"Should I help her?" Ezra whispered as he broke away from the kiss. "Do you want me to help her make you come so hard you black out?"

Oliver couldn't speak now. Coherent language was all gone. He jerked out a nod and Ezra smiled before he began to kiss a trail down Oliver's body. It was too much, it was everything, and

Oliver stared as the two of them tangled their tongues together over his hard cock, shiny from Anna's work at him.

"Keep going," Ezra urged her as they broke their kiss. "But don't let him come until I tell you."

She nodded, her pupils wide and filled with pleasure. Pleasure at doing this to Oliver. For Oliver. He realized that and was moved by it. Almost as much as he was moved by the pleasure she caused when she put her mouth back over him. Ezra shifted her gently, giving himself room at Oliver's aching cock. He smoothed his fingers over Oliver's balls and Oliver choked out a moan in the quiet of the room.

Anna answered it with a groan of her own, humping at the bed like she was seeking her own pleasure. Like this brought her to the edge. And he could see how hard Ezra was too. How much this excited them.

"Give in," Ezra whispered yet again before he gently sucked one of Oliver's balls into his mouth.

Oliver's hips jolted upward as pleasure so intense it bordered on pain spread through his veins. Molten lava that touched every part of him and increased when Ezra chuckled, vibrations humming through Oliver's skin.

Anna began to move her mouth faster, sucking him harder, swirling her tongue around him as she moaned and murmured her own pleasure. The two of them were dragging him to the edge, in tandem, blasting him apart like some exploding star and he did what he'd been told over and over.

He gave in. He surrendered everything in him that said he needed to give, to serve, to earn this pleasure and their attention and their love. He gave in to the sensations and the emotions that these two startling, beautiful people offered. The pleasure arced and he cried out as wave after powerful wave washed over him.

He exploded and looked down to watch Anna take every drop, pumping his cock with her hand as the pleasure ricocheted through him. As Oliver flopped back on the pillows, lazy, sated pleasure making him weak, he watched as Ezra dragged Anna toward him and kissed her. Like he wanted Oliver's flavor. Like he was hungry for it.

Oliver sat up on his elbows to watch them. To drink in their passion for each other, stoked higher by their passion for him.

"I want you to come together," he grunted out. "I want to watch you."

Anna broke the kiss and looked at him, a wicked angel fallen from heaven itself. She shifted herself closer to Ezra, her breasts flattening against his honed chest. "You want to watch him make me come?"

Oliver jerked out a nod. "Please."

"Well, your wish, my beautiful sweet, is most definitely my command," Ezra said as he cupped Anna's backside and wrapped her legs around his waist, rubbing his hard cock against her wet entrance as she arched against him like a wild thing in heat. "Shall we give him a show?"

She glanced up at Oliver and smiled. "Oh yes. I think so. Now."

CHAPTER 12

Anna

Anna had made love to Oliver while Ezra watched over the days they'd spent tangled in each other. She'd made love to both men together. And she had watched the two of them as they explored each other.

But this was the first time she would only touch and be touched by Ezra. And the idea of having all his intense focus spiraled in on only her was thrilling.

The idea that Oliver would watch their every move, even more so.

Ezra laid her on her back on the mattress at Oliver's feet, letting her legs dangle off the edge as he eased away from her and took a place standing between her thighs. He pushed her open farther, his bright blue eyes sparking in the firelight. They were filled with as much promise as his touch when he swept a finger across her entrance. He lifted the digit and showed her the wetness there, proof of how aroused she had become while pleasuring Oliver.

He smiled and then turned toward Oliver. "Taste what you do to her," he ordered and leaned over toward him.

Oliver opened his mouth and sucked Ezra's fingers inside. Anna found herself lifting her hips, staring mesmerized as Ezra thrust his fingers into Oliver's mouth like he would his cock.

At last he popped his fingers free and looked down at her. "I don't think it's fair that I don't have a taste too."

He dropped down, pushing her thighs open with strong hands, and licked her in one hard stroke. She gasped at the pleasure of his hot mouth and ground up into him as he sucked her clitoris lightly.

"Mmm, so sweet, Anna," he purred against her. "So perfectly sweet, I could just eat you all day and all night."

He rubbed his cheek against her thighs, abrading the skin lightly with the rough evidence of stubble and then burrowed his mouth against her a second time, his tongue pressing into her, thrusting there a moment before he let it trail up to circle her clitoris again.

The last few days had made her so aware of her own pleasure. It had stripped away any hesitations she'd ever had to take what she wanted. After all, both these men seemed infinitely excited by her pleasure. Seemed driven to chase it, draw it from her, let it stimulate them as she came.

And oh, but she wanted the pleasure this man would give. Over and over. Already it was mounting, and she shut her eyes to enjoy the sensations he brought washing over her. She let her mind wander, merging Ezra's touch with memories of having Oliver in her mouth, of his groans of pleasure, of the taste of him when he fully surrendered and called out her name as he came.

She jolted, her orgasm hitting hard and fast and deep. Wave after wave washed through her entire being and Ezra was relentless, sucking her clitoris, pumping two thick fingers inside of her as she came. At last he moaned and lifted his head, watching her as she panted with relief.

"Gorgeous," he murmured as he leaned up over her, caging her body by placing one hand on either side of her head. He pushed her legs wider and she lifted against him, taking his thick cock into herself.

She would never be accustomed to the stretch of either of these amazing men. To how good it felt to be filled up with them. Even if she had the pleasure of being theirs for the rest of her days.

That moment drew her back to reality. Back to the fact that forever wasn't promised by either of them. Her future was still down the road, miles away, with a man who would not care about her pleasure. She shivered as she fought to forget that and focused instead on the moment she was in.

Ezra's brow wrinkled as he stared down at her. "Don't go far away, Anna," he murmured before he leaned down to kiss her. He was gentle, caressing her with his lips, then probing softly with his tongue that tasted like her release.

She lifted into him, wrapping her arms around him and reveling in the comforting weight of him. He drove against her once more, pivoting his hips in slow circles and she ground against him, seeking more contact between his pelvis and her sensitive clitoris.

The pleasure he'd built with his tongue returned, but slower. A burn that came from deep within her soul, that spread throughout her body like she had a whole lifetime to nurture it. She began to shake, pulling back to watch him.

His gaze was focused on her, he held it there without hesitation and she drowned in him as she quaked and gripped her thighs around his hips while she rode the pleasure he brought her.

"Yes, yes, yes," he murmured, his strokes growing harder, faster as he lost himself. But he never broke their eye contact, not until he threw his head back with a harsh, heavy moan and filled her with himself.

At last he collapsed down over her, raining kisses down

against her neck, against her collarbone, whispering sweet empty words against her skin as she mewled in pleasure.

"God, but that was sweet," Oliver whispered, threading his fingers into her hair.

She jolted at his touch and smiled up at him. The moment between herself and Ezra had become so intense that she'd surrendered herself fully to it. But knowing Oliver had been watching them made it even better.

Ezra shifted off of her and she crawled up beside Oliver, resting her head against his shoulder, pressing kisses to the skin there.

Ezra moved too. He lay his head against Oliver's stomach and immediately Oliver began to gently stroke his hair. She sighed as this feeling of complete safety washed over her. It was nothing like anything she'd ever known before. And it was because of them. These two remarkable men who gave her more than plea-sure. They gave her everything.

She sank into that realization, closing her eyes and letting herself slip into slumber. Soon enough she would wake. Not just from her dreams but to a reality where this time ended.

And the future she dreaded would come to pass at last.

Ezra

Anna whimpered softly and Ezra lifted his head to look at her. She was still sleeping. Dreaming. Though perhaps not the happiest of dreams when it came down to it. He looked past her and found Oliver watching her just as closely, his full lips pulled into a frown of concern.

"When this is over, she'll be lost," Oliver whispered so as not to wake her.

"I'm paying her for posing for me," Ezra reminded him gently. "She won't be without funds."

"It won't be enough," Oliver said, his voice rough, just as it was always rough when he talked about any danger to Anna. "*He* will make sure it isn't."

Ezra stiffened. "The new duke. Her late husband's uncle."

Oliver hesitated a moment and Ezra held his breath. This man had protected Anna's secrets for the entire time they'd been here. If he surrendered them now, it meant something. And he wanted Oliver's trust. He wanted to earn what was so carefully given.

At last Oliver nodded. "Yes. I realize men like you don't like to see the worst in each other, but the new duke is a monster and will destroy her if he has to, in order to gain power over her and her...her..."

"Body," Ezra said mildly, though the idea of Anna in such a situation made him feel such a deep anger. Such a savage sense of protection that he had to meter it.

Oliver paled. "Yes," he whispered, and gently rolled Anna away. He was less gentle as he pushed past Ezra and got to his feet. He paced away, toned backside backlit by the fire as he rubbed a hand through his tangled hair. "We shouldn't talk about this here. I don't want to wake her."

Ezra nodded and got up. He motioned to the door. "Then let's talk about it somewhere else. I don't think it's a subject we can ignore any longer."

He picked up his dressing gown and handed it over to Oliver. Oliver stared at the fine fabric with a shuddering sigh. "I... couldn't..."

Ezra snorted. "I had your balls in my mouth half an hour ago. I think we're past little courtesies. Put it on."

Oliver's lips pursed but he did so, and Ezra grabbed his trousers from the pile of discarded clothing on the floor. Together they walked out of the bedchamber and into the sitting room attached. Ezra closed the door gently and motioned to the chairs before the fire. Oliver took one but sat on the edge, as if he was uncomfortable. Ezra shook his head. It seemed the man would always revert to the role of servant, no matter what wicked things the three of them shared on his bedroom.

"What do you know about the new Duke of Sedgewick?" Oliver asked.

Ezra shrugged. "Not much. I have separated myself from my father and grandfather's world for a long time. By choice."

"Well, he is…" Oliver bent his head but there was no hiding the rage in his expression. It rippled through his entire being from his clenched jaw to the way his fingers flexed in and out of fists against his thighs. "He is what I already declared him to be: a monster."

"He wants her," Ezra said softly.

Oliver nodded. "Yes. He always wanted her, even before his nephew's untimely death. The way his eyes would track her, the way he would find ways to touch her under the guise of assistance or care…I could have killed him."

The emotion in Oliver's voice made Ezra shift. It was so very evident how much this man loved Anna. Loved her deeply and passionately and with a purity that made Ezra's scarred soul think of summer days. It made him think of possibilities that he'd believed were lost a long time ago. Oliver challenged his bitterness and stone walls and everything else about himself.

So did Anna. And that was slightly terrifying, but also exciting.

"Because you wanted to protect her," Ezra said softly.

Oliver nodded slowly. "Yes. But I couldn't. Not from the pain caused by her husband. Not by the danger posed by his uncle. You two want me to pretend I have a power I don't, and it is a beautiful little fantasy. But there is no place I feel more powerless than when I watch her hurt. When I watch her fear. When I watch her cry and cannot do anything to build a wall between her and those who would hurt her. Because I *am* a servant, Ezra, whether you two suck my cock or not. I'm a man with no power, no means. And this fantasy world won't change that. Not in the long term."

Ezra let out his breath softly. Oliver wasn't wrong. It was almost impossible to change the station to which one had been born. To fall was easy. To climb…well, it took a great deal of privilege and money and work to do so. There were few who made it.

"If the money isn't enough, what would be?" Ezra asked. "What do you think would protect her?"

There was a long pause and Oliver dropped his gaze away from Ezra. He stared at the floor, as if the expensive carpet was the most interesting thing in the world. When he spoke, his voice trembled. "Marriage. He couldn't touch her if she married someone with power. Someone like…like you."

Ezra collapsed back in the chair as the suggestion ripped through him. He'd avoided marriage all these years, unable to fathom giving his life to someone else, not in the way they deserved. Not after Beatrice. But when he thought of Anna at his side, Anna in his arms, Anna in his bed forever…it wasn't something that made him hurt. A surprise to say the least.

"Marry her." He let the words roll off his tongue, measuring their weight and taste.

Oliver's nod was shaky. "If…if you think you could protect her. Love her…because she deserves to be loved."

Ezra slowly leaned forward and covered Oliver's hand with his own. He felt Oliver tense beneath his fingers, his gaze flitting away. "*You* love her."

There was a pause that felt like it lasted an eternity as Oliver struggled with what to say, but then his low, rough voice said the one syllable that could change the world, that had been changing the world for thousands of years.

"Yes." Tears filled his dark eyes, tears of despair and tears of joy. "Yes, I love her."

～

Oliver

Oliver heard the words from his own lips, the ones he had fought for years not to say, not to feel. And they burned him, destroyed him. He loved her and he knew it didn't matter, not really. Not in the end.

"And yet you would surrender her," Ezra said, his fingers tightening against Oliver's, offering solace and understanding. He knew what it was like, after all, to lose someone he loved. The circumstances were far different, but the end result would be the same.

"Because I love her," Oliver whispered. "*Because* I love her, I would give up everything to see her safe and happy and taken care of. I would give my life for that."

"To earn that from you is a glorious thing," Ezra said softly, and for a moment they only held stares.

Oliver felt the yearning in this man. The loneliness that he hid behind the casualness of his easy command of everyone around him. But Oliver knew better. He knew Ezra needed and deserved to be loved. What was more surprising was that he wished he could give that to him. Longed to spend the time and energy it would take to dive deeply into this man's life and soul and come out drenched in him the same way he was drenched in Anna and all the little secrets of her spirit.

Ezra's brow wrinkled like he recognized the connection they could forge and almost...feared it. "I know I care for Anna. And I can feel how that could develop into love. I also know she has begun to care for me."

"She has," Oliver said with certainty. "I have watched her for too many years not to know the signs."

"Even when they're directed toward you?" Ezra asked.

Oliver let his eyes squeeze shut again and relived every moment he'd ever shared with Anna. From the first moment he'd met her to the moment just a short time ago when she'd looked up at him, dark eyes wide with desire and care as she pleasured him. Oh yes, she loved him. That fact might have actually made all this worse.

"Will you do it?" he choked out. "Would you marry her and protect her?"

Ezra hesitated. "Yes."

Relief and heartbreak flooded Oliver in equal measure. There would be no place for him if Ezra followed through on his promise. He couldn't imagine serving the house of his two former lovers, watching them fall in love and Anna forget whatever warm feelings she held for him.

Or worse yet, maintain them and feel her eyes follow him when he came into a room. That had been hard enough when he didn't yet know her taste or the feel of her arms around him.

"Good," he said. "You should arrange it as soon as possible. Take her to Gretna Green if you can. Just do it before the new duke can do anything to harm her. Just marry her."

"I beg your pardon."

Both men looked up and Oliver caught his breath. Anna stood in the doorway between the sitting room and the bedchamber, a sheet wrapped around her full curves. She was staring at them and her eyes flashed with anger. She shook her head.

"Just who the hell do you both think you are, making plans about my future without even consulting me?"

CHAPTER 13

Anna

Anna's heart pounded as she stared at her two lovers, seated close together, hands intertwined. She would have loved that image of the two men had she not overheard at least part of their schemes.

Ezra rose. "Anna, I understand now what you are fleeing from. What was driving your desperation. You cannot deny that a marriage to me *is* a good answer."

She continued to look at Oliver, not Ezra. "So you two just decided, after all you've seen me go through, to make this decision and plan out the steps."

"You're angry?" Oliver said, and had the gall to sound confused.

"Yes!" she cried out, moving toward them. "How could I not be?"

"The new duke is dangerous," Oliver said, slowly getting to his feet. She heard the soothing tone to his voice, the one that had comforted her so many times. The one that called her to him, made her want to curl into his arms and just let him fix everything.

"He is," she agreed. "I'm no fool. I know he has stripped away all hope I have for independence so that he may hold my life over my head. I assume he would demand I become his mistress in exchange for my financial security. He is disgusting and the idea of his touch makes my stomach turn."

Ezra's cheek twitched with anger, but his voice was still calm when he said, "And I could protect you from that future. If you were my wife."

She let herself look at him. This man had been a stranger less than a week ago, and yet now she could easily picture a life with him. One of creativity and laughter, passion and respect.

But that wasn't enough for her. Not now that she'd felt the pleasure of these two men. Not now that she could admit how much she loved Oliver.

"I don't want to be without…without either of you," she admitted. "So that is why I'm angry. You would make your plans without even taking into account that I…" She faced Oliver slowly and cupped his chin, making him look at her, *see* her. "I love you, Oliver. I love you with all my heart and any arrangement that left me without you would be untenable."

She glanced at Ezra, hoping that this admission didn't hurt him. But he was smiling just a little, like the thought brought him joy. So she refocused on Oliver and found his expression more muted. Pained.

"I couldn't give you what he could, Anna," he whispered. "Don't you think that I'd want to? That I would give you the world if I had it in the palm of my hands."

"You silly man," she murmured, stepping closer, putting her arms around him and not giving a damn that her sheet fell and she was doing this as physically naked as she was emotionally. "You *are* the world."

She lifted her mouth to his and he didn't resist her. He let her kiss him. He made a soft sound in the back of his throat and he kissed her back. Passionately, powerfully, without holding back even a little. She felt him pour his love into her, his heart, his soul and tears streamed down her face as she accepted it all with all she ever had been and ever could be.

"She loves you, Oliver," Ezra said, settling his hand on her lower back. Oliver seemed stunned, as if hearing it once, twice, was finally breaking through his shell. But Ezra spoke again, so he didn't have to. He pivoted Anna gently, so he could look at her. "And I know that you and I both feel that same spark between us. The beginnings of something beautiful. And I feel the same with Oliver. This is not one love, one choice. It is a love that is between us all. As a threesome, as each individual couple. Or am I wrong?"

"No," Oliver answered, his voice trembling. "I…I do feel something powerful for you, Ezra. Deeper than desire."

"Much deeper," Anna added.

There was relief on Ezra's face as he leaned in, and suddenly all of them were kissing. Mouths and lips and tongues colliding together as they held each other.

Anna didn't know how long it lasted. A moment, an hour, it didn't matter. When they all touched, she lost herself. She never wanted to be found again. But at last Oliver was the one to step away. He sighed.

"So what do we do?" he asked.

Ezra smiled. "You two liked the painting I did of you together?"

Anna blinked and glanced toward Oliver, who seemed as confused by this change of subject as she did. "Y-Yes," she said.

"Good, because I would like to paint a series of you two. Of we three," he said. "I want to paint a dozen portraits that capture the power of what you two do to me. And when it is done, I want to exhibit it. In very special places. If you would agree."

Anna was still confused, but she could only imagine how

wonderful the posing sessions would be for such a thing. "I-I would like it."

"I would, too," Oliver said slowly. "But how would that solve our problem."

"Well, my manager of affairs and his wife"—Ezra looked back and forth between them as he spoke—"would need to stay with me. Under my protection. I would need to paint you two, after all, and train Oliver in how to manage an artist's schedule and… appetites. Though Oliver is already very good at the second." He leaned forward and kissed Oliver.

Oliver returned the kiss and then pulled away, blinking. "Manager of affairs," he repeated blankly. "And his wife."

"Marry Anna, if she would agree. If she would have you." Ezra took her hand and set it in Oliver's. And you would still have my protection. And my passion. And my love as it grows and multiplies and makes everything between us richer and better."

Tears stung Anna's eyes at that utterly perfect resolution. She squeezed Oliver's hand lightly. "Don't be my servant anymore, Oliver. Be my equal. My husband. My sun and moon. My world."

He was staring at her, his expression unreadable. But then the corner of his lips twitched in a rare smile. One that grew and broadened and seemed to brighten everything around them.

"You are my world," he whispered. "But are you certain you'd want this? It would change everything."

"Everything was already changed the moment you touched me at the Donville Masquerade," she said. "The moment our carriage stopped here and you brought us to Ezra. I wouldn't go back. Not for all the gold in England. Not for anything in the universe." She rested her hand on his chest. "Will you marry me?"

She glanced toward Ezra and brought him forward. "Will you *both* make me yours not just body but in every way that matters?"

"Oh yes," Oliver said.

Ezra slipped his arms around her and drew her between them

so they could both embrace her as they also touched each other. "Oh yes," he echoed. "In every way that matters. Forever."

Anna was shaking as they held her, touched her, moved their way back to the bedroom where they would consummate these promises over and over again. Tears streamed down her face as she realized that from the deepest sorrow had been born the greatest joy.

And she would never stop celebrating that, or these amazing men, until the day she drew her last breath.

EPILOGUE

Six Months Later

Oliver

"I'm sure you can make room on Mr. Pembroke's schedule for *one* showing at my establishment," the man standing before Oliver begged, batting his eyelashes as if he could seduce the yes from Oliver.

And while he was very handsome, Oliver only had eyes for two people amongst the writhing bodies in the crowded hall at the Donville Masquerade. He smiled across the room at Ezra and Anna, who were standing with the proprietor of the club, Marcus Rivers and his wife, Annabelle. They were all talking to the patrons who wished to look at the erotic art that was on display in the wicked halls of the notorious hell.

Oliver had already arranged five more private commissions from the work and negotiated three sales of the pieces Ezra was able to part with.

"I will speak to Pembroke," Oliver said to dismiss his companion. "Perhaps I can persuade him."

The gentleman smiled knowingly. "I would wager you could. You have my card."

Oliver nodded, but he was already moving across the room toward his wife…and his husband. After all, he and Anna had been married months before at Gretna Green. And just last week they had shared in a similar, private ceremony with Ezra.

In the months since their being stranded at Ezra's home, Oliver's life had entirely changed. He loved them both to distraction, and he was confident in his occupation, thanks to Ezra's training. He didn't feel like a servant anymore, and as he grew more comfortable in surrendering himself, Ezra and Anna had showed him how much his trust could be rewarded.

Now his mouth watered as he reached them just as Rivers and his wife stepped away to speak to more of their patrons. He slipped an arm around Anna's waist and just barely resisted the urge to kiss Ezra right there in the middle of the hall.

"Bloody hell, but you are popular," he said.

"You make that sound like a bad thing," Ezra said with a chuckle as he traced Oliver's fingers with his own and sent a shock of awareness through him.

"It's not," Oliver said, his head spinning. "Though I do have some interesting news."

"What is that?" Anna asked.

"Rivers' man of affairs and I were chatting right before the opening and he said the Duke of Sedgwick tried to break in to get a glimpse of the paintings early."

Anna's smile fell. "What?"

Oliver nodded. "He made such a scene that he was tossed out on his arse in the alleyway by three very large, rather unpleasant men. It's a huge fall from grace because it happened in front of at least a dozen patrons waiting for proper entry. There are whispers amongst the crowd that he has already been uninvited from at least three upcoming social events."

"Good," Ezra said with a dark expression. "It couldn't happen to a nicer fellow. Let him burn alive in the heat of his jealousy and bitterness."

Anna let out a sigh of relief. "He doesn't even matter anymore," she said. "You two made sure of it."

Oliver could see that the relief was real. He and Ezra had worked hard together to protect their wife. He smiled and changed the subject to relieve any lingering anxiety the subject caused. "At any rate, with how popular you are after this grand opening, Ezra, I'm going to be rearranging your schedule for a week trying to fit in all the people who want a taste of you."

"No one tastes him but us," Anna teased.

Ezra shivered. "Indeed. But if we are to tour these beautiful images, there *will* be some advantages. Fucking in the carriage. Fucking behind screens. Fucking in the halls of very powerful people."

Oliver felt his cock getting harder with every lewd suggestion. "That is true. Anna, do you think you're up for it?"

She smiled as she reached out to cup each of them through their trousers. "It seems both of you are. May I suggest we retire to a back room and have a little fun?"

"Oh no," Ezra said, taking her hand and then Oliver's. "One dark hall and the moans of others seems like the perfect way to celebrate."

Oliver laughed, desire and peace somehow merging within him, giving him a joy he never would have thought possible. "I would very much like that."

"So would I," Anna said, and together they stepped into the same darkened hall where he had pleasured her so long ago. To repeat that night, only this time with even more love, even more desire and the knowledge that he never had to let her or Ezra go again. That their lives were permanently merged, happy for the rest of their days.

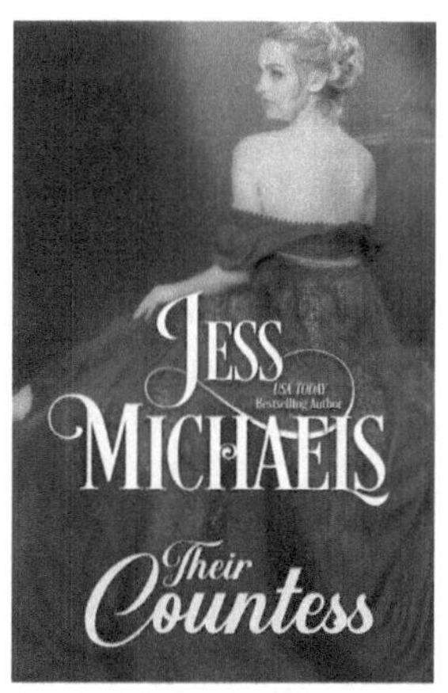

Order Now!

Richard Fitzroy had been acutely aware of the gorgeous couple he had just watched fuck on the settee from the moment they had entered the ballroom hours before. Not only were both of them stunning, her with her honey hair and bright blue eyes, him with that broad shouldered confidence and angled jaw that seemed ripe for tracing with a finger…or a tongue, but there was something else.

They didn't belong at this gathering. No one else seemed to have noticed and Richard wasn't in the business of outing anyone. So he'd just watched them. As they separated and paraded around the ballroom, drawing everyone to them like flies to honey. He'd watched them come back together from time to time, too, the sexual energy between them so palpable that it made him sweat a little. Made his palms itch with a desire to get closer.

It had been a long time since he'd wanted anyone. Anything. He fucked from time to time, of course. He wasn't a monk. A night at a house of pleasure with a man or a woman…or both… scratch an itch the same way eating food fed an empty stomach. But it was all rather…rote.

This draw to the strangers in the ballroom was different. Powerful. He'd fled it, taking refuge in the quiet of a sitting room only to have the pair intrude, not noticing him slouched in a chair in the darkest corner of the room, nursing a scotch. Not noticing him as they drowned their desire in each other.

And revealed the true nature of their attendance tonight.

They were thieves. Richard supposed he could march back into the ballroom and reveal them. Perhaps others would have done so out of some class loyalty. But he felt little of that. He'd grown up with and around the fools in that ballroom. He knew that on the whole they deserved anything that knocked them down a peg.

He pushed from the chair in the corner of the room, feeling the throb of desire their display had caused easing and the cock-stand that had leapt up demanding attention softening. He could go back into the ballroom, at least. He could watch them some more, this time with a different eye.

He strode down the hall, smoothing his jacket and calming his breath as he reentered the ballroom. He gazed across the room immediately, finding the man…Hux the lady had moaned at the height of her passion.

Hux.

He was tall, very tall, with a wiry frame and broad shoulders. He had to be at least three inches taller than Richard and yet he moved with an untamed grace. Like he owned the room. Owned anyone in the room.

As if he felt Richard's stare on him, he turned and their eyes met. Richard couldn't breathe as those dark eyes held his for a beat, two. Hux had crinkles around them, like he smiled often. He wasn't smiling now. Oh, no, he was looking at Richard like he was something…sweet.

Richard swallowed and let his gaze flit down the other man's body. Now Hux did smile, just a fraction, before he turned away and moved into the crowd. Richard felt a strange sense of disappointment. Not that he had any idea what he'd wanted the man to do otherwise. Come over? And what? Steal *Richard's* pocketwatch?

A flicker of idea passed through his mind and then he shook it away. He was addled by this heady desire he felt. That was all. And it was in his best interest to just leave.

But as he turned to do so, he saw the woman of the pair moving toward him, her gaze lit with interest just like Hux's had been. Zara, he thought she'd been called. Zara. A beautiful name. One he could easily imagine himself moaning like Hux had moaned it earlier.

"Good evening, sir," she said as she stepped up beside him.

"Miss," he said softly. They stood for a moment, staring out over the ball together. "I don't think we've met before."

"I would remember," she said with a smile that stopped his heart for a moment. Good God, but she was a lovely creature.

"As would I," he breathed, his voice rough. "I'm Richard Fitzoy."

She inclined her head. "Zara Cooper. A pleasure."

Had she emphasized the word? He couldn't tell if he'd imagined it or if it was real. He felt like he was a little drunk, standing here beside her. Knowing that her partner was circling probably watching them as he'd been watching every man she'd stood beside during the night.

And even though he knew all their attention was likely a way to lighten his pockets, he didn't step back. "Are you enjoying the gathering?" he asked.

She nodded. "Indeed. It's been lovely. And you?"

He glanced at her and cleared his throat. "I…I fear I do not have the temperament for such things. I attend almost against my will."

Her brows lifted at the honesty of the statement. He was a bit surprised by it, too. He knew Zara wasn't here for any good purpose and yet he'd told her a truth he generally kept to himself.

"That doesn't sound like much fun," she said softly. Then she leaned a little closer. "You shouldn't do things that don't make you happy, Mr. Fitzroy."

Order Now!

ALSO BY JESS MICHAELS

Theirs

Their Marchioness

Their Duchess

Their Countess

Regency Royals

To Protect a Princess

Earl's Choice

Princes are Wild

To Kiss a King

The Queen's Man

The Three Mrs

The Unexpected Wife

The Defiant Wife

The Duke's Wife

The Duke's By-Blows

The Love of a Libertine

The Heart of a Hellion

The Matter of a Marquess

The Redemption of a Rogue

The 1797 Club

The Daring Duke

Her Favorite Duke

The Broken Duke

The Silent Duke

The Duke of Nothing

The Undercover Duke

The Duke of Hearts

The Duke Who Lied

The Duke of Desire

The Last Duke

The Scandal Sheet

The Return of Lady Jane

Stealing the Duke

Lady No Says Yes

My Fair Viscount

Guarding the Countess

The House of Pleasure

Seasons

An Affair in Winter

A Spring Deception

One Summer of Surrender

Adored in Autumn

The Wicked Woodleys

Forbidden

Deceived

Tempted

Ruined

Seduced

Fascinated

To see a complete listing of Jess Michaels' titles, please visit:

http://www.authorjessmichaels.com/books

ABOUT THE AUTHOR

USA Today Bestselling author Jess Michaels likes geeky stuff, Vanilla Coke Zero, anything coconut, cheese and her dog, Elton. She is lucky enough to be married to her favorite person in the world and lives in Oregon settled between the ocean and the mountains.

When she's not obsessively checking her steps on Fitbit or trying out new flavors of Greek yogurt, she writes historical romances with smoking hot characters and emotional stories. She has written for numerous publishers and is now fully indie and loving every moment of it (well, almost every moment).

Jess loves to hear from fans! So please feel free to contact her at Jess@AuthorJessMichaels.com.

Jess Michaels offers a free book to members of her newsletter, so sign up on her website:
http://www.AuthorJessMichaels.com/

facebook.com/JessMichaelsBks
instagram.com/JessMichaelsBks
bookbub.com/authors/jess-michaels

www.ingramcontent.com/pod-product-compliance
Lightning Source LLC
Chambersburg PA
CBHW061454210726
48287CB00007B/2510